M000028208

About the author

Cori Melvers is a scientist, writer, and author of the new novel, *Chloe's Catch*. Trained as a researcher and healthcare professional, Cori spent her time reading and writing articles and chapters for textbooks. After years of reading mysteries and other pop culture genres, she is now telling her own stories about smart women with strong character and a dark sense of humor. She has her own dark sense of humor that is a defense mechanism developed from years of working with the public. She is passionate about good pizza and has a soft spot for German shepherds. She has lived in multiple regions of the United States and has travelled around the world, providing education to professionals, and sightseeing. She is settled in South Florida, one of her favorite spots on the planet.

This is a work of fiction. Names, characters, businesses, places, events and incidents are either the products of the author's imagination or used in a fictitious manner. Any resemblance to actual persons, living or dead, or actual events is purely coincidental.

CHLOE'S CATCH

CORI MELVERS

CHLOE'S CATCH

Vanguard Press

VANGUARD PAPERBACK

© Copyright 2022
Cori Melvers

The right of Cori Melvers to be identified as author of
this work has been asserted by her in accordance with the
Copyright, Designs and Patents Act 1988.

All Rights Reserved

No reproduction, copy or transmission of this publication
may be made without written permission.
No paragraph of this publication may be reproduced,
copied or transmitted save with the written permission of the
publisher, or in accordance with the provisions
of the Copyright Act 1956 (as amended).

Any person who commits any unauthorised act in relation to
this publication may be liable to criminal
prosecution and civil claims for damages.

A CIP catalogue record for this title is
available from the British Library.

ISBN 978 1 80016 295 2

*Vanguard Press is an imprint of
Pegasus Elliot MacKenzie Publishers Ltd.*
www.pegasuspublishers.com

First Published in 2022

**Vanguard Press
Sheraton House Castle Park
Cambridge England**

Printed & Bound in Great Britain

Dedication

Dedicated to all the smart women who raised me, and to my friends whom I could not make it through life without.

Acknowledgements

Thanks to LCD for reading and providing direction when I need it.

Prologue

"Chloe, come back here. This is the last time I am going to rescue anything, let alone a dog with long legs." Panting, and distracted by her need to catch Chloe, she ran right into a hard object. Sarah touched the object and slowly looked up into bright grey eyes alerting her to the fact that she did not just run into a pole or a building. The man with rock hard abs, who was tall, had brown hair with a touch of silver at the edges, and was holding on to the end of a leash, grinned at her despite his annoyance. On the other end of that leash was Sarah's German shepherd puppy, Chloe.

"Excuse me; I was chasing her and didn't see anyone standing in front of me."

"Of course you didn't," declared Dirk. "I'm Dirk and you are welcome. What are you doing letting a puppy run down the streets in this neighborhood? She might run into the street and in front of a car!"

Sarah put on her best smile. "Thank you." She was sure if she said anything else it would offend the man who had just saved her from a mile run. The thoughts and images that flashed through her mind were conflicting. On one hand she wanted to kiss him, a long sultry kiss, not just a 'thank you for rescuing my puppy' kiss. On the other hand, she wanted to kick him for admonishing her for letting a dog run loose. Like I had any choice, Sarah thought to herself but then said, "Chloe is a rescue, and she is only a year old. I have been training her and thought I had made big strides. Apparently, I have not. She saw a cat and took off. Again, I am so sorry for running into you. I need to get going."

Sarah looked up at Dirk and found herself looking directly into the eyes of her newest obstacle. Dirk seemed to have purposely planted himself right in front of her and was smiling at her as he blocked a quick escape. Saying thank you a second time, Sarah was thinking that he would move. He was still holding the leash. She looked back up into those grey eyes and knew for certain this was a man she would meet again under different circumstances. Her intuition was never wrong. She didn't really know how to proceed, so she took Chloe's leash from him and instead of finding out where he lived or how to get a hold of him, she walked away. She forgot to give him her name.

Dirk watched her go and wondered if he would ever see her again. He was hopeful but remembered after she was too far down the sidewalk that he did not get any details, most importantly her name. He vowed to find her. Even if it meant he would be walking up and down this street until the next time she was doing the same.

Sarah was running late because Chloe had decided on a whim to chase a cat. Now that both were on the right ends of the leash, they headed toward *Iguana Meet You Café*, the cafe on the corner of Alhambra and Douglas in the Gables. When they got there, Kathy was already seated at an outside table and was sipping on a diet cola. January in South Florida was a good time to sit outside; the weather was cool and there were not many bugs. Today the sun was shining, the temperature was seventy degrees Fahrenheit and there was a slight breeze. A perfect day for lunch with a friend.

"Sorry we are late; Chloe got away from me. I think she ripped my arm off."

"Your arm looks perfectly well attached." Kathy flashed an evil smile.

It has to be her naval training, thought Sarah as she grabbed her seat on the patio with Kathy. "What's up, you still thinking about poisonous plants?"

Kathy had already ordered lunch for the two of them. That way she made sure Sarah stuck to her salad plan; only because Sarah made her promise, otherwise Kathy did not really see anything wrong with Sarah's appearance. Kathy thought she was beautiful. But she knew that Sarah would not be attracted to her. So, she kept her feelings to herself, and was happy for their friendship.

"I ordered our lunch, and I really want to talk to you about this case I have been assigned to crack. You have to promise me that you won't tell anyone else about it."

"I promise to give you Chloe if I let out any information."

"I don't think that giving me your first child will be necessary; I just want you to understand the seriousness of this case."

Crossing her heart and raising her hand in a Girl Scout honor and grinning, Sarah said, "Okay, I understand how serious it is, and I promise to do my best. Are you going to deputize me, like they do in the movies?"

"You watch too many movies, Sarah. No, there is no deputizing and there is not really anything that I think will be dangerous to you. But I do need your plant and poison expertise."

"Oh," Sarah's lip stuck out and she wiped away pretend tears followed by another giggle, "You know I am not a toxicologist; they are the ones who investigate the effects of chemicals, and drugs on the body and study the treatments. I am not sure if I can help with poison. I am kind of disappointed though; I was hoping I would get to do something adventurous. I have not had any adventures for a while. My life is boring these days. Life as a professor is not all glitz and glamour like people think. Although, I might have run into an adventure this morning. But first tell me about the case."

Kathy leaned forward and quietly began. "There is a serial killer loose in South Florida."

Louder than she should have, Sarah yelled, "There's a what, a serial killer, and you said there isn't any danger to me? Who are you kidding?"

"Sarah, keep your voice down; luckily it's just us on the patio, but really, I need this to be kept quiet. I need your help, but I really have to be sure that you can handle this?"

"Okay, I am just a little surprised, because of all the things I think I can help you with, it is not a serial killer. Maybe a cereal killer, because you never know what they are putting in those breakfast foods these days. In fact, eating cereal is on the decline, so maybe the question is who is killing the cereal?"

"Really, Sarah? This is not a time for puns, no matter how much you love them. I am being serious. I need your help."

"Okay, so tell me the story."

Kathy looked around to make sure that there was no one else in hearing distance or watching what she was doing. You could never be too cautious. "Sarah, there is something or someone killing people and it occurs to me that they might be using a plant, or natural medicine to do it because the coroner keeps reporting natural causes, but there is something wrong. I think they have been poisoned. I was watching 'Arsenic and Old Lace' last week."

"Aha, I knew it."

"Here is what I know. There are twenty-five persons who have died in approximately the last twelve months and our unit has been asked to investigate this, and now me specifically. The coroner did not find anything on autopsy, except that all the individuals reported symptoms of headache, flu-like symptoms, and leg pains and some changes to their fingernails before dying. They were all in the same hospital in South Miami."

"Kathy, none of that sounds particularly suspicious to me. People die every day. Why does anyone think that this is a serial killer, or even murder?"

"That's a good question. There are some similarities that the coroner noticed and brought to my boss. Those similarities are the symptoms reported by these individuals, and they are men and women who are over seventy years old; they all died after they got to the hospital. They had high potassium levels. Does any of that make any sense?"

"Kathy, that makes even less sense that there is someone murdering these people. High potassium levels will stop the heart if they are high enough. I don't see how I can help you."

A man and woman in their mid-fifties walked out on the patio and sat down beside Kathy and Sarah. The man looked nervous and like he would rather be anywhere but on the patio at the Iguana. The woman with him was wearing a ring, but she also appeared nervous.

"Maybe she isn't his wife?" Sarah grabbed Chloe and craned her neck, investigating the couple further.

The couple were talking quietly among themselves and the waitress went over to take their order. Chloe wriggled away from Sarah in order to meet the newcomers, and took off, over to their table.

"Chloe, come back here and sit." Sarah ran to catch her before she could get away from the restaurant. Sarah apologized that Chloe bothered them, but Chloe wouldn't stop growling at the man. "I really am so sorry; she is just a puppy and she just would like for you to pet her. We'll be leaving shortly, so sorry to bother you."

The woman introduced herself as Mary Pinter and said that she loved dogs, and asked about Chloe's age, and where did Sarah get her? Sarah introduced herself to Mary, but the man never gave his name. Sarah asked if they lived in the neighborhood since the Iguana was basically a local dive, and the tourists didn't tend to stop.

"Sarah, we moved to the neighborhood about a year ago from Ohio after some job changes. We are so glad to be living where it is warm, and to meet new people. I hope we will see you again here."

"I am sure we will; this is a favorite haunt for Chloe and me." Sarah directed Chloe back to the table and sat back down with Kathy.

"What was that all about?" Kathy asked.

"I am not sure; Chloe is still barking at everyone, but she didn't seem to like him. Mary said they moved here a little over a year ago. She did not say anything else, except to ask about the dog. She also said they come in here often so we may see them again. He seems to be the nervous type. Let's get back to our discussion of death and plants."

"I would rather not continue discussing this now. Just think about it, and get back to me. Maybe at another place we can discuss it further."

Both women got up to leave; Chloe led the way.

Sarah headed out on the one-mile walk to her house with Chloe, thinking about all that she and Kathy talked about. It was interesting to think that twenty-five people had died, and that Kathy felt there was a connection to medicinal plants. Sarah worked on a list in her head of all the things she needed to think about, and the research that would need to be done in order to help Kathy. She had no idea of a place to start. She also found her mind wandering to thoughts of Dirk. How would she find him?

Where It Begins

The Defense Safety Administration, or DSA, was part of the United States Department of Justice. There were offices in large cities across the United States with mandates to investigate crime, protect the US citizens from corruption, and to enforce controlled substance laws, among others. Detective Kathy Doe worked for the Miami-Dade County office which was located in downtown Miami in the old Dade Commonwealth building across from the port. The DSA was created in the early part of the century. Many government offices, including the Environmental Protection Agency, the United States Institute for Peace, the National Park system, Federal Bureau of Investigation, and the Drug Enforcement Agency had been eliminated in efforts to reduce the size of the government. The DSA was formed when the US Congress created it as an independent agency. Congressional members expanded the limits of oversight to include Internet of Things (IoT) and drug-related crimes. This last mandate kept the DSA Detectives in Miami-Dade County Florida remarkably busy.

Kathy had arrived at work on the previous Monday morning to several messages on Viber, her phone light was blinking signaling she had messages, and over a hundred email notifications beamed from the computer screen.

This is what she got, she thought, for not looking at her phone on the weekend. She refused to give up her few unscheduled weekends to this place. They got all the rest of her time. She couldn't have a dog; She was gone too much. She didn't like cats even if they did prefer to be at home without her. Her thoughts were interrupted as her colleague Trina popped her head into the cube and related that the boss was waiting to see her.

"I'll be right there. I am going to get some caffeine, and a donut. I can see it's going to be that kind of day."

"I'll let her know." Trina left and headed back to her desk.

They had just gotten a new boss assigned to the Division. Janine, the new boss served as a JAG. The Judge Advocate General's Corps (JAG Corps) was the branch or specialty of the military concerned with military justice and military law. Kathy was hoping to build a relationship with Janine based on that shared history. Kathy's other hope was there would be less micromanagement around the office. The old boss had burned up the Viber at all hours of the day and night. Kathy grabbed a diet cola and a Krispy Kreme from the kitchen and headed to Janine's office. She knocked on the door and got an "Entrez vous."

Kathy entered the office with the hope that the whole conversation wasn't going to be in French. She was not sure she was up for it at seven thirty in the morning, even though Kathy was fluent in several languages, French being one.

"Good morning, Janine."

"Buenos dias; sientate, por favor," responded Janine.

Kathy concluded that Janine was either testing Kathy's language skills or showing off. It did not matter which it was to Kathy, because this early in the morning she just wanted to drink her cola and eat her crème-filled donut.

"I was notified by the director at Mercy Hospital that there are eight more victims of alleged poisoning in the past three months that she believes all experienced the same cause of death. Even the coroner is not sure exactly what it is. It appears to be a virus that attacks the nervous system."

"Well, in that case why is the DSA being called in to investigate? This seems like an epidemic of disease, and there is reportedly an outbreak of the H1N1 virus in Florida. The Centers for Disease Control and Prevention is the organization that should be called in to investigate." Kathy bit into her donut, while she watched for Janine's unspoken response.

"That is what it looks like at first glance, and Doctor Canon did call the CDC. The investigators from the CDC said they didn't think it was a virus. But then again, they didn't know what the HIV virus was in the early days either. Let's hope we don't have that kind of thing breaking out again."

"Let's not go down some strange path this early in the morning. What do we know?"

"We know that in approximately the last twelve months, we have twenty-five people all over the age of seventy who seem to have been healthy active adults that died within a few days of being admitted to the same hospital with flu-like symptoms and pain in their legs. The doctors provided supportive therapy and did blood tests, but nothing unusual showed up except for a high potassium level. One question is why do they all have high potassium levels? That is what I have. I am reassigning this as a high priority case for you and want you to figure it out and identify the problem before there are any more dead bodies."

"Look, Janine, this really seems to me like it isn't in our purview. I am not even sure where to start. What is a high potassium level? If you give me crimes that involve illegal drugs being smuggled in by airline flight attendant mules, or human trafficking, it is much easier to follow a trail and figure out where to start."

"You start eating an elephant one day at a time," answered Janine.

Kathy left Janine's office shaking her head and wondering why she had been assigned to 'eat an elephant' on a Monday morning. When she got back to her desk, she went through her emails. "Nothing there, except a bunch of notices from human resources about policies for this thing and that, mostly saying be nice, don't screw with your cube neighbor, and next Monday is a holiday," she said to herself.

She hit delete on all one hundred emails and thought, that takes care of one thing. I hate emails.

Kathy checked her Viber app and there was nothing interesting there either. She moved on to the blinking phone. There was only one message, from a girl who had been stalking her since Kathy met her on a date two weeks ago.

She must have pulled a card from Kathy's pocket because she really didn't remember giving her, her number. That was sloppy of her, very sloppy. She did not have time or patience for a relationship unless Gertrude Stein showed up. She might consider a relationship with her because she is just so interesting. She was fairly sure she was dead, so back to the problem at hand. Where would she start?"

The phone rang and it was the coroner.

Kathy and Sarah

Kathy had lived in South Florida since the last big hurricane went through and ripped up Coral Gables. She purchased a fixer upper because the people who owned the house left it, collected the insurance money and did not come back. She settled into the neighborhood and for the first time in a long time, maybe even since she served in the Navy, she felt like she belonged to a community.

Kathy grew up in New York, and her parents moved her around a lot. She went to a few different universities including Columbia, New York University and Fordham before finishing her degrees. She never liked sitting in a classroom, but her parents were determined that she would get a degree. She went through more majors than she did schools before she finally decided to get a political science and law degree. She graduated from Fordham at the top of her class. From there she joined the Navy because it fit her adventuring spirit. She completed officer candidate school and went to JAG. When it was time for Kathy to leave the service, she found a job with the government and lived in several places around the world. Kathy spoke English, Spanish, French and Farsi. Kathy was

24

six feet tall, had dark skin, dark hair and dark eyes and was considered beautiful by most who encountered her. Occasionally people asked her if she was a model. Sometimes she replied with the answer, "No, I am a circus clown." The looks on their faces and their responses made her laugh. The thing about that response was that some days being in her office at the DSA felt exactly like that.

Sarah was a pharmacist and pharmacognosist whose home in Coral Gables was south of the airport and she had lived there for several years since taking a faculty position at the University of Miami. Sarah attended the University of Toledo in Spain, and Comenius University in Bratislava. She loved to travel and had been all over the world, sometimes as a tourist, sometimes as the expert speaker on a panel regarding medicinal plants. She spoke fluent English, Slovak, Spanish and French. Sarah was fair-haired, had dark eyes and described herself as needing to lose a few pounds. She worked out at the gym and she got a puppy for company but also to keep her walking. Sarah admitted to being in love with romance even though that part of her life hadn't always gone so well. When people made fun of her, she responded with, "A person can be a scientist and romantic. They are not mutually exclusive." Sarah worked hard, she was fun, and she liked to have fun. Often, she was not taken seriously because of her blonde hair and being overweight for most of her life. It used to bother her that no one took her seriously; now she owned every inch of her being and brains, and spent her energy working to make life better for others whenever she could.

Sarah met Kathy at the gym one day when they were both lifting weights, and in Sarah's case, trying because in her opinion the ones she used were far too unwieldy. One day, after a few weeks of working out together, while discussing backgrounds and experiences, Kathy and Sarah discovered a few common interests including solving puzzles.

Kathy began their conversation one afternoon by asking Sarah about medicinal plants. "Sarah, what kinds of plants are there that can be used to kill people?"

"Well, there are quite a few. There are also other poisons that are not from plants. Did you watch 'Arsenic and Old Lace' or another murder mystery on TV, that you would ask me a question like that?"

"I am pondering a case and I could use your help, if you are interested."

"Yeah, I'm interested. Tell me about it. How do you think I can help? Was someone really poisoned with plants?"

"Let's not get ahead of ourselves. I'll meet you tomorrow and we can discuss it. I don't want to talk about specifics in a place where we have to talk over workout equipment."

"You haven't told me exactly what you do. You just said you investigate crime. What company do you work for?"

"If I told you that, Sarah, I'd have to tie you up and keep you from the public forever, so you don't tell anyone."

"Ha, ha." Sarah then saw the look on Kathy's face. "Wait, you are serious? You can't be serious. No one says that and means it."

"I do. I'll see you at the Iguana Meet You Café tomorrow for our very first spy meeting." Kathy laughed at the incredulous look on Sarah's face. Kathy reflected that it was worth going to hell for lying, just for that look.

The women walked out of Star Fitness to their respective vehicles. Sarah headed home to let Chloe out before she went to the university. Kathy headed to the morgue.

Dirk Can't Get Her Out of His Head

A week later Dirk was having dinner with his friends at Monty's. The tiki bar was a great place to catch up with people on a week night and feel like you were in the islands. The drinks were great, the scenery wasn't so bad, and the music was a cover band named Port-of-Call that played '80s music. Dirk and his team were gathered around the bar watching the band and drinking mojitos.

Dirk ran a tech company called BOTS with administrative offices in downtown Miami on Brickell Avenue. He designed smart applications in the early '80s for houses. He often lamented selling that patent for way too low a price because now there was a smart device in almost every house in the United States.

He had moved on to designing personal assistants for the blind. His EYE BOTS as he called them were in testing and service in multiple states. The EYE BOTS could identify and complete simple household chores, make calls, identify and pay bills electronically and carry out simple commands. The company was doing well: it had enough investment funding to keep developing for the future and revenues were good. Dirk felt like he was on top of the business world. Now, if he could just get the rest of his life in order and his mother to quit asking him for grandchildren... Dirk described the girl in the street to his friends to see if anyone recognized her. No one did.

"I really hope to find her again, but I have no idea how or where to start."

"Why didn't you stop her?" asked his best friend Dave.

"Because he wasn't using the brains in the head on his shoulders when she ran into him," replied Gina.

Gina Portense was a vice president in the company and responsible for marketing. For a moment in time, she thought she and Dirk might hook up. Then she realized that it probably wasn't a good idea and stopped flirting, for the most part. Gina had been waiting on Dave to ask her out for a long time. She didn't know if it was the company rule that kept him from asking, or something else. Gina liked to give both Dave and Dirk a hard time about women, and tonight was no exception.

Dirk laughed and said maybe she was correct this one time. "Dave, buy us another round; it's your turn, because you asked the last stupid question of the day."

Dirk, short for Dexter Irwin Keene, found himself consumed with thoughts of the girl and her dog, Chloe. Her smile and the way she ran into him and just stood there so close, and the scent from her cologne aroused feelings that he had not had in a while, as well as stirring a part of his anatomy. His fiancée had left him standing at the altar two years ago and he still didn't trust women, or his heart. His fiancée had called him from her cell phone. She was in the back seat of a taxi leaving the church and said that she couldn't marry him because she was in love with his brother James. James was his best man and was standing next to him when Laura called him to give him the news. He turned and punched James in the face, just as they walked out, in front of the guests. Dirk was remembering all of this and it made him laugh. His mother was screaming at him during the wedding fiasco, his father was laughing, and all their friends and relatives, all three hundred of them, looked aghast. It really was funny, and he hadn't been able to laugh about it up to this point.

"Hello, Earth to Dirk. What are you thinking about?" asked Gina. "It can't be that you are that absorbed in the music; they aren't that good and about every other song is disco music. They aren't even as good as the Weather Girls. What are you creating in that head of yours?"

"Oh, sorry, Gina. I was thinking about the wedding that didn't happen. My brother still hasn't forgiven me for breaking his nose; plus, he lost the deposit on the tuxedo."

"I really don't think it's your brother who should be forgiving anything. He slept with your fiancée, and then he married her the next week after she dumped you at the altar. Worse, he married her in a courthouse in the Bahamas on your honeymoon package."

"Yeah, well, I dodged a bullet on that one. She is crazy, and she keeps him on a truly short leash. I don't have time for that. But I do have time to find that girl and her dog."

Gina shook her head in disbelief and ordered another mojito.

Name That Plant

Sarah woke up and took Chloe for a short walk and then took a shower so that she could get ready for work. It was a short drive over to the university from where she lived, but traffic was nasty in the morning and even though she could put the top of her cherry red '65 Mustang down and enjoy the weather, it was still a hassle putting up with the honking and the yelling and the brandishing of guns if you got in the wrong lane at the wrong time. She smiled, thinking about the fact that she was here in paradise and could drive to work and enjoy the warmth of the morning sun while doing it, rather than focusing on the negative. Sarah finished dressing for work and headed out the door. She told Chloe to guard the house and that she loved her. Sarah wondered to herself if dogs ever hear more than blah, blah, blah when you talk to them. But she kept doing it because after all, Chloe was family.

While on her way to the office, Sarah began to ponder the conversation she had with Kathy about the poisons. Even though Sarah was not a toxicologist, or someone who studied poisons, she was a pharmacist. She was licensed and could practice at the local Walgreen's. She preferred to study the medicinal properties of plants and contribute to research on new drugs. Herbal medicines had become extremely popular in the last years, and there was so much that the public did not know. One thing Sarah hoped was, in this case that Kathy was working on, that the pharmacist would not be the bad guy.

She was so tired of the pharmacist being the one who poisons people, or who is giving the poison to the murderer. In just one story on TV or in books, she would like to see the pharmacist solve the case. The high potassium levels in these people who died was like what happened in a Desperate Housewives episode several years ago. The pharmacist was jealous and put potassium tablets in the husband's heart medication and the husband had a heart attack. How could one person kill twenty-five people for jealousy? There had to be another explanation.

Sarah arrived at the school and found her parking place. Sarah was too warm and already sweating as she headed across the half-mile distance to the doors of the building. Class started in an hour, so that gave her some time to ponder today's topic, poisonous plants. Sarah headed to her office to complete a little bit of research.

Sarah arrived at her classroom with minutes to spare. "Good morning, everyone. Today, I want to deviate a bit from the syllabus and think about plants as poisonous rather than pretty and smelling good. Let's start with hearing from you what plants you think about when I say 'poisonous'."

"Poinsettias are poisonous to dogs."

"Foxglove can be poisonous; I saw that on TV," retorted Gary, a good-looking man who came back to the university after many years as a high school science teacher. He was tall, built like a basketball player and had a smile as wide as the Amazon River, and was friendly to everyone in the class.

Sarah smiled, thinking it was likely he knew that from years of teaching botany, but if he wanted to be a wise ass, she would give him a pass today.

"Right, what about a popular tree that grows in South Florida and many people put in their yards for the beautiful flowers?"

Charleen Parker, also a student who came back to school after years of working, responded with the answer, "The angel trumpet tree — I believe that is what you are asking about. All parts of it are poisonous; there have even been reports of teenagers trying to crush it up and use it to get high. They died."

"Very good, Charleen. You are exactly right. Thank you. I'd like all of you to review the plants that we have discussed so far this semester and determine what the effects are when used in humans in native cultures or processed into medications by manufacturers. Are these effects beneficial, or do they cause harm, if used in human consumption? It is important to think about all the properties of a plant, not just those that we use for helpful purposes. In your role as a pharmacognosist you will be asked your opinion about the use of plants in certain cultures or ethnobotany, and about using them for purposes of treating disease or maintaining wellness. You will also have questions from people about plant use for pets as well as humans. Please put your thoughts together in a posting on Course4Me for everyone to see, and respond to, by the end of the week. If you go to post about a plant and someone else beat you to it, you will have to find another plant."

The students let out an overwhelming groan.

"It's fair; first one to write gets their pick of plants. Everyone must respond to at least three posts from a classmate. I hope everyone has a good afternoon. I'll see you next class. You know how to get a hold of me in Course4Me if you have any questions or want to set up an appointment." Sarah headed for the door with a wave.

Back in her office, she faced her desk. One day she would clean it, but today wasn't that day. She sat down and reviewed her emails. Nothing important in there — just whining from the dean and the department chair. All of that could be dealt with later. She checked her phone for texts and there was one from Kathy.

Kathy: Meet me at the gym tomorrow morning?
Sarah: Sounds good to me, eight AM, c U then.

I wonder if she has more dead bodies, or more evidence? Sarah reflected on their conversation and was jarred from her concentration by 'Mamma Mia' playing on her phone, indicating a text from her mother.

Mom: Do you gnaw on bones for dinner?
Sarah: Mom, you really have to read your texts before you send them. I am not sure what Do you gnaw on bones for dinner means?

Pondering, Sarah returned to the murders — to her two dilemmas. How would she help Kathy when she was not sure these people had been murdered? She seemed convinced there was something wrong. How would she find Dirk? Where should she start?

A search of the literature revealed several possibilities for poisons that could be used to kill a person and go undetected, but most were not derived from plants.

Arsenic was one option; it was a metal. Though it didn't cause flu-like symptoms or a rise in potassium, so that might rule it out as a cause of death. Many people don't know that arsenic was used in make-up for many years as a coloring agent. It was still allowed to be used in make-up in the US in small amounts. Another culprit, the mineral potassium, had been used to poison people because in high doses it stops the heart. It seemed unlikely that people would have gone to the hospital with flu-like symptoms and been given overdoses of potassium there, or was that a possibility? Maybe if they were dehydrated, and someone used potassium instead of sodium chloride by accident. Sodium chloride is what is used to rehydrate people. There have been criminal cases where hospital staff felt like they were helping people who did not have any family by sending them to a premature grave; maybe someone was substituting the potassium on purpose. Oh, that was so creepy; could there really be someone at Mercy Hospital killing the elderly?

Sarah turned her thoughts to Dirk and blushed even as she debated the soundness of trying to find him. She had been on a path to the Iguana Café and Chloe had caused them to deviate. If she went back to the same place, about that same time of day, would she find him?

Sarah reflected on the whole situation and how Dirk had changed her perspective. She had been married briefly to a caring, wonderful man and that had ended in tragedy and heartache. Her husband was killed in a boating accident almost four years ago and she had not really been interested in anyone since. She had not felt like looking at anyone else at all. Dirk was the first man that had even caused her to have any feelings. Chloe was there in Sarah's imagination while she was trying to figure out the Dirk dilemma.

"Chloe, you ran south on Douglas instead of north toward the Iguana. Was Dirk coming from the Tri-Rail train and walking home; does he live in the neighborhood? So many questions, so little evidence to help find him. Chloe, you are being no help. I wonder if he is on Facebook." A quick search on her phone revealed that there were a little over three hundred Dirks and she did not have a last name. Some of them did not have photos. This was not helpful. Sarah started a search for Dirk on the internet. That was futile.

She turned her thoughts back to the alleged murders. Sarah closed the computer, picked up her things and headed out to get Chloe for a walk and maybe some Chinese for dinner.

A Day in the Life of Harold and Mary Pinter

Mary and Harold Pinter were sitting at the breakfast table discussing work. Harold and Mary had been married for over thirty years and had four married adult children and twelve grandchildren. Mary worked at a local lab and was doing research for OptyX, a company that made optical instruments. She was lucky to have gotten this position in Florida as a relocation. She had been with the company in Ohio for over twenty years. When she and Harold suddenly found themselves needing to leave Ohio, she was glad they found work here. Harold was a massage therapist, although he came to that profession after retiring from the post office. He was a mail carrier for many years and was laid off when the industry was privatized. He liked to give Mary massages and so she encouraged him to go back to school and get the license to become a massage therapist.

"Harold, what does your schedule look like for the week?"

Harold, failing to put down the article he was reading, responded, "It's pretty full but I think I have time to come by the lab and see my wife for lunch. I haven't been there for a while and I could use a look at your pretty face more often."

Harold suffered from depression and had been taking imipramine for many years. He did not really think he needed it, but it did help him sleep at night. Mary had pushed him to the brink several times, and he would leave her but after thirty years, he needed her, if for nothing else, the stability that their marriage provided him. Mary also pushed him to get help for his 'depression'. There was not much help for people with depression, he thought, because after he had gone to three therapists and two psychiatrists, he still felt depressed. He felt he was missing something in his life, but he did not know what it was exactly.

Harold tried several medications over the years, and most of them gave him side effects that he did not like. He tried Prozac when it was new in the '80s. It made him hard for hours which hurt like the dickens. Mary joked about it, but she did not understand how painful it was. He was not even feeling affectionate when it happened; it just happened. Once it happened when he was with a female in a massage session. She complained to the manager and he had been fired. There was no recourse for him. She had been an older woman, and he tried to explain that priapism was an adverse effect of his medication. Once his boss found out he was taking medications for depression, she let him go. What had happened to being protected if you have a disability? He guessed depression was not considered that kind of disability. He still did not understand, with all the things that were blamed on depression, why the government didn't do something about it. After the incident with the woman and the massage, news had gotten around his small home town and he had been marked as a pervert. He could not get a job. So, they had to find a place to move and start over.

Fortunately, Mary had been able to transfer to South Florida and he was able to get a job at MassageMe in the Gables. It was a new chain opened to compete with the other massage chains that had gotten so popular over the last fifteen years. He found a new physician in Florida and went back on the imipramine. He was still angry over what happened in Ohio, but he had found ways to deal with it. Mary headed off to the lab and Harold headed off to the MassageMe. They gave each other a peck on the cheek as they left their condo.

"Love you, Harold."

"You too, Mary."

Harold reflected on his marriage while on the way to work. He almost ran a red light, he was so deep in thought. The honk of another driver brought him back in time to miss the car in the intersection. Shaken, but having done no harm to anyone, he continued to the office. When Harold arrived, the first thing he always did was to go over his schedule of clients. Most of his clients were men because many women preferred a woman therapist. He was fine with that. He did not want any more incidents like the one in Ohio. He was just perusing his client list for the day when his boss came out of her office. She quietly told him that the client Jules Verne on the list would not be in. His daughter had called and said that he died the week before.

Harold responded with his sympathy for the family. "He was a lonely man. He had his daughter, but they did not have a good relationship. He often told me he missed his wife who had died several years earlier. I hope he is at peace."

Charleen, one of the other massage therapists, walked to the reception area and saw that Harold looked sad. "Harold, is anything wrong?"

"No, everything is okay. Corina just told me a client of mine died this week. He was a nice man, but lonely."

"Oh," Charleen responded hesitantly. "Do you know what happened?"

"No, Corina just told me that his daughter called and said he would not be in any more. How are you, Charleen? Are you still taking classes at the university?"

Charleen was busying herself with an iPad and reviewing her client list for the day. "Humm, oh yes, Harold, I am still taking those classes at the university. I have about twelve more to take to get my doctorate. Then I will have to spend time writing my final paper. So, I have a bit to go, probably another year or two. The courses are interesting, and there are some remarkably interesting people in my class. I need to go; my first client is here and ready for her massage. See you in an hour and a half."

Harold was left standing in the waiting room because his first client did not show up. He was pondering the death of Mr Verne and wondering where he died and if it had been sudden. Harold speculated about Charleen. She was single. He thought she was nice looking for a woman in her mid-forties. Maybe he is way off on her age, but it did not matter to him. He found her surprisingly interesting and sexy in an awkward way. They got along well, and he often thought about her when he was massaging his clients. He waited for her to walk out of a room after finishing a massage, and he would strike up conversations. She had been working at this MassageMe for the last twelve months. They started about the same time and he felt they were friends. Sometimes they had a drink together after work, even though he was not really supposed to have alcohol. He wondered if she ever had thoughts about him. He knew that the stirring he felt was not a side effect of the imipramine. He was taking a drug called Cialis, much like the little blue pill Viagra but you took it every day, so it was more convenient. His other medicines had made it difficult for him to get an erection with Mary. First it was the priapism, now it was erectile dysfunction or what they call it on the TV commercials, 'ED'. Getting older was not what he expected. He was not sure what he expected, but he knew this was not it. Now, as he was thinking about Charleen, the ED did not seem to be a problem. Just then, the light alerting him to the arrival of his next client buzzed, and he needed to attend to him. Thoughts of Charleen had to wait until a little later. He hoped this client would not notice the rigidness in his pants. He had paid the price before, but for quite a different reason.

Mary was wrapping up her day at the lab. She was responsible for ensuring that the chemical inventory was put away and kept under lock and key. There were certain chemicals that required great caution because they could harm a person if mishandled. One of those was a metal called thallium. It was banned in the United States as a way to kill rodents but was still allowed to be used by industries such as optics and semi-conductors. The lab also used arsenic in the production of their product. Mary locked up the chemicals and left for the day and sent a text to Harold.

> Mary: I am on the way home. What would you like for dinner, my love?

Harold's phone buzzed and he saw it was Mary texting him about dinner, but what he wanted for dinner was not on anyone's menu tonight.

> Harold: I will be home too late for dinner. I'll order in here.

Not a Typical Afternoon at BOTS Inc.

Dirk was in his office, but his mind was elsewhere. His assistant came in with paperwork to sign for the purchase of supplies needed for research. Greta noticed his lack of attention.

"Boss, you seem to be in a faraway place this morning?"

"Greta, thanks for bringing in the paperwork for me to sign. I think there are some forms that need to be run by the attorney. Please ask Pat to look the contract over before I sign it."

"But, boss, you haven't even looked at the papers."

"Let the attorney take care of it."

Greta had known Dirk for an awfully long time. She started as an assistant with him at his first company and had been with him ever since. There was only one other time when she believed he had been this distracted, and that was the week after he was supposed to get married. She felt a motherly affection for him, and so she knew when he needed to talk.

Greta hesitated and then asked, "What's on your mind this morning? Because it doesn't seem to be the development and sales of the EYE BOTS. You are somewhere far away. Are you feeling okay? Do I need to keep people out of your office for the rest of the day?"

Dirk turned his head in her direction and gave his attention back to Greta. "No, Greta, I am fine. I am not building more BOTS now, although we do need to get moving on the idea for the personal assistant BOTS. Have you thought any more about what they need to be able to do?"

"Yes, boss, I have. I think they need to be able to deliver your coffee, tell you when you are being a jackass, and turn off the lights at the end of the day. Will that be all?"

"Humm… yes. Did I say something to offend you?"

Greta was headed through the office door when Gina crossed her path. Gina noticed that Greta did not seem too pleased with whatever had just happened in Dirk's office.

"Good morning, Dirk. How is your day? I heard that we have made progress in Minnesota with the EYE BOT trials. It seems like the biggest problem is that there is an error in the math algorithm, and they are under or overpaying bills. It is no worse than a high school graduate, but still, we need to work on it. I can't market a BOT that cannot do math."

"Well, then you need to find someone to fix it."

"Ummmm, as much as I would like to do that, you do remember that I am your marketing VP, not the algorithm bunny," said Gina, the sound of her sarcasm filling the space between her and Dirk.

That seemed to bring Dirk back from whatever planet he was visiting. "Gina, how would you go about finding someone that you only know what they look like, you don't have their name, but they have a puppy and walk on the same street you take from the Tri-Rail on your way home?"

"Really, Dirk, you are still stuck on that girl? You are the CEO of a successful company, you are sexy, you are smart, and most importantly, you are rich. You can have any woman you want, including most of the employees of this company, and that includes me if you ask nicely." She laughed and continued. "Why are you pining after someone you don't even know?"

"Gina, you understand that I can't date anyone from the company; there would be harassment suits and more if that were to happen. I have extremely strict rules about that for me and for all of you who work with me. A man must keep his hands and eyes to himself. Besides, I think of you like a younger sister; dating you would be against the law in most states." Dirk flashed his best grin in Gina's direction.

Annoyed and steaming, Gina responded, "Why is it that all men now bring up the Me Too movement in a conversation about relationships?"

Dirk let it slide and moved the conversation forward. "Gina, I am serious; I really want to find this woman. I am so desperate I am willing to walk around

47

the neighborhood calling out the name of her dog, which she did tell me; it is Chloe. Her smile is brighter than a falling star, she has this cute little nose, and eyes so blue they could be the ocean and I am falling right into them."

"The dog?"

"No, the girl."

"Oh, please, Dirk, spare me the description, and the drippy romantic blubber of a man who can't have what he wants. We really have more serious things to do than think about a girl," she said, mocking, "with a smile better than a meteor." Gina threw up her arms and blasted, "I have BOTS who cannot do simple math!" Turning red from her chest upward, she stormed out the door.

Gina walked over to Dave's office, hoping to get a little sympathy and some help with the EYE BOT problem. Dave was the engineer who wrote the first code for the BOTS. Now he was doing more in the area of operations than designing.

Who knew how much help he would be? Gina contemplated what she needed to tell Dave when she got there. She thought about what Dave gave up while continuing working with Dirk. Dave graduated from MIT and was one smart dude. He could have been a rocket scientist, and he'd had offers from Boeing, Lockheed and NASA. Instead, Dave followed Dirk's dreams and was here in South Florida designing EYE BOTS that in theory would replace the seeing-eye dog.

Gina was doubtful if that would ever happen, or that BOTS would replace people like Greta as personal assistants, but she supported Dirk's dreams. Gina popped into Dave's office to see if he was free. The assistant was one rude man in Gina's opinion, and she was sure he was one of the seven dwarfs. Why Dave kept him around was beyond her comprehension. She would be glad when they had a BOT to replace him, that was for sure. Gina decided to take her chances and she walked past Grumpy straight into Dave's office. Dave was reviewing a financial sheet but looked up and motioned Gina to come on in, even though she was already in his office and moved to sit down in a chair in front of him.

"Dave, have you had a chance to talk to Dirk this morning? Do you know that he is pining over that woman from the sidewalk? Do you know we have EYE BOTS that cannot do math? What are you going to do about it, and not necessarily in the order I presented it?"

Dave took a deep breath, mentally preparing himself for the Monday morning Gina tirade. It never failed. She came to work on Monday morning, after a weekend with her lousy boyfriend and took it out on everyone else. He had loved Gina for many years, and she was the reason he stayed at the company, in addition to being Dirk's best friend. But she would never know it because he would never have the courage to tell her. However, he was the only one of the executive team members who could handle Gina, and so he would talk her down from this too.

"Gina, Good morning to you too. Why don't you come in and have a seat, and let's talk about what's on your mind?"

Gina was already sitting down, and she got even more agitated. "Do not, and I mean do not, placate me, Dave Johnson. I am a VP and I deserve the same respect as everyone else."

"Funny about that. I am not the one who came into your office unannounced playing a brand-new game of twenty questions. So, I am unsure how it is you think I am placating you. You terrify my assistant, and he is threatening to leave, and he is remarkably good. I would prefer he stays. So, do you want to talk about the BOTS and solve their math inabilities, or do you want to sulk because Dirk is occupied with the thoughts of other women?"

Gina took a deep cleansing breath and looked at Dave. How did he always do that? He was always the one with the cool head, he never got mad, and he always had time for everyone else. "Do you know that the EYE BOTS are having a problem? They are under or overpaying bills, and as a seeing-eye companion, this is an issue. They need to be able to add and subtract! What are we going to do?"

"Tell me the exact issue. Is it in the amount that they are adding or subtracting, or is it in the way they are processing payments?"

"I don't know the difference if you want to know the truth. I am a marketing VP, not a math major. I just know that our customer service staff reported that they had over two hundred phone calls this weekend, and we only have one hundred EYE BOTS in testing or in the marketplace. How am I going to market something that has problems like that?"

"Let me work on it."

Gina continued to sit and look at him expectantly.

Dave looked up from his computer. "Don't you have something else to do? I'll get back to you when I figure out the problem."

Gina left the office without a word. How did he do that? She sent a text to China.

Gina: China can you and Lori meet me at the gym tomorrow, usual time?

China: Yup, I'll text Lori.

At the Gym

Where is Sarah, Kathy wondered? They were supposed to meet at the gym before each of them needed to go to work.

Sarah: Running late
Kathy: you are always late. It's your middle name.
lmao

The naval chief in Kathy wanted to make Sarah do thirty push-ups, but she thought it best to let it slide, and to just appreciate that Sarah showed up to the gym at all. Kathy began to think about the culture of South Florida while she pondered Sarah's late behavior. People in Florida seemed to feel that they were on "island time" even though Florida was technically a peninsula. South Florida was such a diverse community, and that was what made it such a fun place to live. There were people from all over the world; there were a lot of people who left the islands to live on the mainland. Kathy had friends who sent two sets of wedding invitations with different times on them to make sure that their friends who lived on so called island time would be on time to the wedding. Kathy always thought that was a joke that someone made up. It turned out to be the truth. In Kathy's mind, the truth was always stranger than fiction. That thought brought her back to the present, and the case she was working on. You couldn't make up the details of this case. The truth was stranger than fiction,

Sarah arrived and put on workout clothes. They moved to a quiet area of the gym so they could talk about the case. Sarah had done some research but had not been able to find a plant that if used to poison someone would significantly increase their serum, or blood, potassium level. There were plants that were high in potassium, but Sarah didn't think that any of them were the culprit if, and it was a big if in her mind, these people had been murdered. She was hoping that Kathy had more to go on today.

"Kathy, I haven't really found much to go on yet. I started searching but do not have a conclusive idea. I am having a hard time believing that they have all been murdered. I guess that's what makes it a mystery." She nudged Kathy. "Ha-ha, I crack myself up."

"I'll ignore that for the moment, funny girl. I spoke with the county coroner. He really believes that these twenty-five cases are related. He does not yet know how, or why, either. He did some forensic medicine in his past, investigating crimes, as the pathologist for Miami-Dade County, although he is retired from that and now just does autopsies. He says he is willing to leave the investigating to others with more energy. The pattern of these deaths interests him. Since he is the only one to have contact with all the bodies, he felt he should bring it to the attention of the hospital director and urged her to contact DSA. The first body was assigned to him for autopsy about a year ago. He did not think anything of it at that time. The individual was a male, age eighty, but in seemingly good health prior to the hospital admission for flu-like symptoms, headaches and leg cramps. The high potassium level in his blood was treated appropriately according to the hospital records, but the level was high, and the patient expired in two days."

"Did he tell you how high? It matters."

"No, he just said high."

Kathy continued relating the story from the coroner. "He went on to tell me that there seemed to be one or two cases of high potassium-related deaths coming to him a month. He started to be suspicious of something about six months ago, but he couldn't make a case for the murder of a dozen individuals who had all been over age seventy and died unexpectedly from heart failure, because it happens. Then he said about five months ago, a patient who had some other abnormal labs had gone to the hospital and died within a short time. Another coroner did a toxicology screen for drugs and heavy metals. The dead man had a high level of arsenic in his blood. Upon further examination there were changes in the nail bed of the individual. This prompted Doctor Canon to go back through the records of the previous eleven individuals and he realized that some other victims also had nail bed changes, specifically called Mees' lines."

"So, he had one case that he believed to be arsenic poisoning, maybe chronic, and did he report it? Why does he think that the other twelve cases, or any of the last thirteen are related? Did he do tests for arsenic on them? What other symptoms did they have? What did he do about the man who was case twelve and seemed to have been poisoned by arsenic?"

"Slow down, we'll get to that. It's getting a little crowded in here though, and I think we should move to another venue."

The girls got up to go and started talking about the adventures of Chloe last weekend.

Gina arrived at the gym at the appointed time to meet her friend China. They worked out on the weights for over an hour and decided to call it quits. They were in the locker room showering and getting ready to go to work when Gina overheard a woman telling a story that she swore could be about Dirk. She told China to shush and moved closer to the lockers to hear what was being said.

"So, there I am, Chloe is running, and I am running after Chloe and paying no attention to anything but her. I ran right into this man. He was dressed in running clothes, his eyes were the color of the mist when the sun shines through it, he was tall and hot. He had a smug attitude though. I am not sure why I was attracted to him except his body was hard, and he was hot. What do you think?"

"Well, I can understand that you might be attracted to him. You know that he is not my type, so I am not sure I can help you out here. It was a chance meeting on the street; you have no way of finding him. I do not care what your intuition says; you need to leave it alone. At least you know you want to have those feelings again after all these years of avoiding any kind of relationship."

"I don't know, I think I can find him. Maybe if I draw a picture of him and hang it up on the street corners and here at the gym someone will recognize him. Hey, you have artists where you work? Maybe I can describe him, you can get them to draw him, and that will be better than a stick figure that I could draw. We'll add the description and ask 'have you seen this hot, hard man' at the top of the page."

Kathy laughed so hard she hardly got the words out while she caught her breath. "Really, now you have relegated him to criminal or lost dog status. Which is it? You cannot get the artists to draw a photo of him, you cannot hang up his picture and say have you seen this man, no matter how much you might think that is a great idea. I have not laughed this hard at anything for a while. Thank you."

"It is not funny; I do not think he is a criminal or a lost dog! I just want to find him and well, maybe do what dogs do, a little sniffing?"

The girls were laughing so hard that the whole place was looking at them. Even Gina, who gasped when she saw Sarah, and wondered what Dirk was thinking. Gina whispered to China, "That has to be Dirk she is talking about. That is almost the same story that he told us the other night at the bar. He said this blonde with a dog named Chloe ran right into him. He said she was beautiful. I would not describe that as beautiful. She needs to lose a few pounds, and she is loud."

"Maybe Dirk likes his girls with a little extra fluff and maybe he likes them loud, if you know what I mean."

"Really, that's what you have to say; maybe he likes them loud?"

"Well, it isn't like you are ever going to know unless you can get him to break his rule. I think she is kind of cute, but the woman with her is a knockout."

"Oh, don't you start too." Gina threw her hands up in the air.

Gina and China went to the desk to check out after Sarah and Kathy left the gym. Since the gym leadership still had procedures left over from the last century, Gina could check names and numbers.

"There's her name. Sarah Sandling, said Gina."

Gina pointed to the list. There was a phone number as well: 202-765-9087. Gina committed it to memory, but she wasn't sure what to do with the information. On one hand she thought that she could help Dirk if she told him she had found his dream girl. On the other hand, if he found his dream girl, then Gina would not be his only girl any more. Not that she really thought she was, and he had been extremely specific that morning that there would be nothing between them because he thought of her like a sister.

Gina sighed. "I do not think of him like my brother."

"What are you talking about?"

"Nothing. Dirk told me he thinks of me like his sister. How annoying is that? Besides, you know I have been waiting on Dave for years, in truth. I need to get rid of the current boyfriend and maybe Dave will get serious. The clock is ticking."

Sarah reached her car and was getting in when her phone beeped. Once she was settled into the car, she checked her phone.

Mom: Hi honey, Sorry about the text the other day, I told Siri to ask you if you fed bones to Chloe and do you want to come for dinner? I guess she doesn't understand me.

Sarah shook her head and laughed. Technology would never be a second language for Mother but bless her heart, she did try.

Sarah: Yes, mom we will come for dinner, and no I do not give Chloe real bones, except on very special occasions, I give her fake bones.

Desire and Providence

Harold was waiting in the hallway when Charleen finished with her client. He was thinking about her the entire time he had been massaging his client. He knew he should not be having those thoughts about Charleen. He was raised Catholic. He was fairly sure that this fell into the category of impure thoughts and was a sin. Now, as he stood in the hallway waiting for her to say goodbye to her client, he could not help thinking of what it would be like to lay his head on those breasts. How soft they would be. Oh, how those nipples stood out like a lighthouse beam beckoning for him to set them aflame. Harold wondered, would she go along with his plan, or would she laugh and call him a dirty old man? Tonight, he was willing to take his chances. He knew that they were the only two therapists closing the office tonight. They could send the girl at the front desk home, and Charleen could make his dreams come true. They both had one more client for the night. Each massage was an hour in length. Harold wasn't sure how he could stay focused on the client and not think about the pleasures that awaited him, he hoped.

Harold spoke to the girl at the desk. "Please make sure that the clients are checked out before their massage. You can clean up and be out by ten rather than the usual eleven o'clock time."

"Thanks, Harold. I have a test tomorrow and so I would love to leave early. I'll get everything done. Thank you."

Now, all Harold had to do was charm Charleen, and convince her that tonight he was the man of her dreams. Charleen stopped by Harold's room to see him while he was cleaning and preparing for the next massage.

"Hey Harold, are you doing anything tonight after work? I have a lot of adrenaline and think I could use a drink to relax me. Do you want to go over and have a drink at Harry's Place?"

Harold could not think. How had she known he wanted to spend this evening with her? He had such different plans for them. He needed to be cool with his response. "Charleen, I think it will be fun to be together after our last clients. Perhaps there are other ways to relax than going to Harry's but let's discuss it after our clients have gone."

Charleen nodded her head in agreement and went to get her next appointment, who was waiting for her. The client was a woman in her late seventies who just wanted a relaxing massage. Charleen was sure that she would be able to do just that. In the meantime, she wondered what Harold meant. Maybe he would rather go somewhere other than Harry's. It was always a little noisy there when the second shift crowd rolled in. Maybe he needed to talk to her about something urgent.

Harold was so wound up by the end of the hour that he was not sure he could go through with it with Charleen. There was no reason to text Mary to tell her he would be home late because she was always asleep by nine p.m. Their life had become predictable. They worked, they ate, they had the grandchildren over to play when they were on school breaks, and they talked about their children's problems. Sex was a distant memory, not only because of the ED but because when he tried, Mary rolled over and generally said not tonight. He lamented that he did not know when it had happened, but he guessed it happened to all couples. It seemed like the longer you are married, the more you live like roommates and the less you live like lovers. He wanted a lover; of that, he was sure. He knew that was the missing element in his life. Finally, it was time to wrap up the massage and get this man sent home to whomever or whatever it is he was going to.

"What are you doing when you leave tonight, Jack?"

"I've just married a woman twenty years younger and I am going home to practice making babies."

Harold smiled, because that was just what he had planned as well.

Harold watched as Charleen provided the woman she had given a massage to water and sent her on her way. He was cleaning up his room and Charleen came in to tell him she would be just a few minutes. "Do you know that Tracy is already gone?" she asked.

"Yes, I do know. She has a test tomorrow and I told her if she would check out the last two and clean up in the front, she could leave at ten rather than eleven."

Harold slowly moved closer to Charleen as he explained about Tracy. He stood face to face with her as he finished his last sentence and reached up to caress her cheek.

"Charleen, you are a beautiful woman. How often do men tell you that?"

"Not in an exceptionally long time, Harold. What are you doing?"

"Charleen, for several months I have been admiring you, and falling in love with you. I have not had the courage to say anything until tonight. I want to lay down with you and caress those lovely round breasts and kiss your neck and make my way down your body with kisses and pleasure you in several different ways. I sent Tracy home so that we could stay here, and I can make love to you."

"Harold, I don't know how to say how flattered I am but let me try. Harold, you are a married man. How can you possibly have fallen in love with me? You don't know anything about me, and I don't know much about you other than your favorite sports teams."

Harold placed his hand on her breast, caressing her nipple. He pulled her closer to him, wondering if she would resist. When she did not, he placed his lips on hers and slowly and tenderly kissed her until she responded. He moved Charleen with him to the room next door. Before his last client he had lit candles and placed the vibrator that they used for muscle tension relief in this room so that he could massage her in ways that he hoped would make her moan with delight. He had been hearing it in his head for months.

"Charleen, I don't want to do anything that you are not comfortable doing. I have been waiting and thinking about this moment for several months although I have been afraid to approach you. You are a beautiful woman, and I want to make love to you. Do you want to make love to me?"

It had been a long time since anyone paid this kind of attention to her. Charleen was overwrought with the emotion of the moment and a tear or two ran down her cheek. "Yes, Harold. Oh yes!"

She reached out and took his face in her hands as he did with her earlier and kissed him until he gently slid his tongue between her teeth and tasted her anticipation. He laid her down on the bed and slowly and methodically undid the buttons of her blouse until he released her breasts from the confines of her lacy bra. He stared at the beauty of them and the perfect shape. He leaned over to suckle them and heard her first cry of delight of the night. Charleen was already gone; she released a sigh as he nipped and sucked. The sounds she was making were music to his ears. He carefully started the vibrator and ran it at a slow speed down each one of her legs coming back up between her thighs.

Charleen moaned. "Oh, Harold, please don't stop."

Harold continued to massage her gently up and down her legs, between her breasts and over her belly. The sighs of delight made Harold harder with every passing second. He wanted to bury himself between her legs, but he did not want the night to end just yet. He needed to slow down, or he was going to explode far too soon, and he wanted to ensure that he spilled every bit of seed he had into her tonight.

Harold stopped the vibrator and moved his hand to gently massage her. Charleen quickly removed the rest of her clothing because his touch was so gentle, and so warm. She wanted a man to take her in his arms and love her. Tonight, Harold became that man.

Charleen had seen some very rough days in the last couple of years and she found ways to deal with her anger and hurt, but this, this was heaven. Harold continued to caress her, and she continued to respond to his touch in ways he had never been able to imagine. Why had he waited so long? Finally, as Charleen was begging him to fill her up, he could no longer resist her pleas.

Harold laid down on his back on the second massage table and began to stroke himself so Charleen could watch. She was glued to the sight of him as he pleasured himself for her. He invited her to be on top. Charleen was so wet, and so wound up that she wasn't going to argue about positions at this time, even though she had other preferences. It had been so long, and she was so needy that she gently climbed on top of Harold and slowly slid down onto him and grabbed on to his shoulders and covered his mouth with a kiss. She slowly moved to the rhythm that Harold was setting and in a short time, they both exploded with spasms that went through each of them like fireworks, something neither of them remembered having felt like before.

Charleen moaned his name. "Harold, Oh, Harold, you have made me so happy and this feels so good; please don't stop. I want more of you every night."

"I can't believe it, I haven't had an erection for the right reason in a long time, let alone one that resulted in this much ecstasy. I don't know if we can manage every night, but I want to be with you whenever we can work it out."

He was spent and as Charleen draped her body over his, they fell asleep in each other's arms. Later when they awoke, neither wanted to leave. They knew they must clean up the place and go their separate ways. It was hard parting, but they left with a promise on their lips that tonight was the first, and not the last night they would be together.

Meanwhile, at the Morgue

Kathy and Sarah agreed to meet at the coroner's office that afternoon, once Sarah finished with her class and had a chance to appease her department chair who wanted some strange report. Sarah walked out of the chair's office and was on her way to meet Kathy across town. On the way to meet Sarah, Kathy looked at her texts to discover that there was another hospital admission from last night. The hospital director had set up a system of alerts in case another individual came in with flu symptoms and headaches. The woman had arrived at the ER early in the morning.

Kathy: there is another hospital admission.
Sarah: So where do you want me to meet you, the county morgue or the hospital morgue?
Kathy: stick with the plan see you in 30.

In all of Sarah's years of adventure she had never had one like this. She had rowed two hundred miles down the Amazon River, but that seemed like a walk in the park compared to the excitement of this case. Investigation was not what she had gone to school to do specifically. But, as a young girl, she read Nancy Drew and Encyclopedia Brown, and this was exactly what she wanted in her life right now.

She was so thankful to have met Kathy. She knew she was going to be fun that first day in the gym when she had laughed at her when she dropped the weights. These chance meetings lead to good things if you just trust your intuition. Sarah wondered about Dirk and if her intuition was right. She had better get to the morgue; Kathy would be waiting. It would be just fifteen minutes if she didn't run into any traffic.

Sarah parked her car and headed into the morgue. Kathy was already there.

"You beat me here. What is new, you always beat me everywhere. One day I'll surprise you and arrive early, maybe."

"Hi, Sarah." Kathy led them in the direction of the coroner's office.

"So, is she dead?"

"Is who dead?"

"The woman you said the director called you about?"

"No, Sarah, she isn't dead yet, but based on previous cases, she doesn't have very long."

"Oh, that's so sad. It seems like we should be able to help her. I really have no idea where to start, Kathy. Is the medical director having the doctors do heavy metal labs, and labs for drugs like opiates?"

"Yes, I am told that is their procedure since the coroner alerted them to the arsenic."

"Here we are; shall we see what we can get from Doctor Canon?"

"The coroner's name is Doctor Canon?"

"Yes, Sarah, and don't start with 'it sounds like a made-up name' or saying something like he must be a real ball to talk to!"

"Now you are catching on, Kathy. That is not exactly what I was thinking, but it will do for now."

"Sarah, what possessed me to talk to you that first day in the gym?"

"Sheer madness, I suspect." Sarah laughed.

Kathy opened the door to the coroner's suite and entered with Sarah in tow. The women were welcomed by an assistant who said that Dr Canon was expecting them, and they should go straight back and turn right into his office. Kathy knocked on the door of Dr Canon's office and he waved the women in and gestured for them to have a seat. He was just finishing a phone call that looked like bad news. They continued to stand.

"Good afternoon, ladies. Thank you for coming by. That was the hospital director and Mrs Ruth Morgan died just before lunch. She will be on her way here shortly. She is toe tag twenty-six in this strange unfolding of events. They sent the heavy metal tox screen for testing, but we will have to wait for it to come back."

Kathy wanted to get a few questions in before Sarah started with her list. "Doctor, when did you or the

68

hospital staff start doing heavy metal toxicology screens on individuals?"

"That is a good question. We do not always do them, but in the case of number twelve, I had an itch at my intuition and so I had the screening done. It turned out that was correct, and there was a high level of arsenic as I have already indicated to you."

"Have you started doing them on everyone now since number twelve?"

"Excuse me," interrupted Sarah, "Does number twelve have a name? These are still people we are talking about."

"Says the woman who wants to hang up signs looking for a man like he is a lost puppy."

"Ladies, if we might stay on task, please. Yes, number twelve's name is Daniel King. His case was suspicious because he did not seem to have the same social history as the others. He had a wife. The others were widowed or widowers if my memory serves me correctly. I thought perhaps their spouses had been involved in their deaths. But since they did not have spouses for the most part, then I thought it seemed to be cases of contracting a virus. Mr King had the same symptoms, but as I said, my intuition had me doing the extra lab testing."

"Should he really be part of this whole investigation, or is he an outlier and a case of murder the police should be investigating?" inquired Kathy.

"That my dear, is also a good question. I believe they are all related. I have been doing heavy metal screens on all the victims since Mr King, or they were done in the hospital."

"What have you found?" Sarah plopped down across from Dr Canon.

"The funny thing is that I found arsenic in two more of the victims but not everyone."

"How do you know that all twenty-six are victims of murder?" asked Kathy who took a seat as well.

"Well, I don't. But I called in the Centers for Disease Control and Prevention or the CDC first, thinking that this was an influenza epidemic. But that was not until after about case number five or six. These people have all been old. Well, old is relative when you are looking at your seventieth birthday as I am in about a month. Let's say they have all been long in the tooth, to use an incredibly old expression. After case number five, I called the CDC and their physicians examined the next few cases. We did influenza testing on all the first five or six before they were cremated. The testing is not a hundred percent accurate after death, but there are studies that give it about a fifty percent accuracy. I started testing the next few deceased who came in from Mercy Hospital with similar medical history and social histories. I got nothing.

"The CDC examiners said 'They aren't dying from influenza; maybe someone is killing them'.

That gave me pause because I had not really thought that to be the case. By this time, we were up to victim number eleven. So, when victim number twelve, excuse me, Mr King, was brought in, I tested him for opiates, which was not valuable because he had received pain medications in the hospital, heavy metals, and other drugs. The results as I mentioned indicated a high concentration of arsenic. By the time, the results were back, there were more deaths. I did heavy metal testing on them and came up with nothing on two. But then two more individuals after Mr King, according to my notes, had high levels of arsenic."

"What metals are tested for in a usual heavy metal toxicology test?"

"That is a good question, Doctor Sandling. They are lead, mercury, arsenic and cadmium. There is so much mercury in the local fish that many people have high levels of mercury here in South Florida. But that is not the case with any of these individuals, at least not high enough for that to be the cause of death."

"Doctor, I'll need a list of the twenty-six deceased names, their nearest contacts, the cause of death that you assigned, any testing you did on them and any statements or records from the hospital that might be useful."

"You will have to get the patient records from the hospital. I can give you their names and personal contact for the next of kin listed. In some cases, they are not family, but a friend."

"Doctor Canon, I am a pharmacognosist, not a toxicologist so am a little out of my league here. I know there aren't too many tests for specific plant toxicities because there are so many, but did you do digoxin levels which comes from foxglove on these pati—er... victims, or insulin? When did the high potassium levels make you suspect?"

"Those are more good questions, Doctor Sandling. The labs are done upon admission to the Emergency Department or ED, and then daily while they are hospitalized. I have to admit though that I did not do digoxin levels postmortem and I do not believe that they were done in the hospital since the patients were not reported to be on digoxin."

"Thank you, Doctor Canon. I think that is all the questions I have for now."

"I will follow up with you to get the names and contacts by the end of the day. I will call the director to get the records of the deceased individuals. I will be back in touch soon. Let us know what the cause is for this afternoon's death," said Kathy as she stood and moved toward the door.

Kathy led Sarah out of the door and into the halls before she said anything. She was thinking about how this case was stacking up, literally. There were twenty-six bodies, one who was clearly poisoned, and twenty-five others who did not seem, on the surface, to be murders. She still did not know exactly what she was looking for, but it was looking more and more like it

72

could be a serial murderer, who may have had compassion in mind.

"That was a good suggestion about the digoxin, Sarah."

"Well to be honest, I doubt that is the case. There is something we are missing, but I am stuck."

"Join the club. Let's get a late lunch and figure out the next steps."

Where There's Fire

Gina had been pondering what to do for several days. She didn't have any reason not to tell Dirk what she had learned at the gym, but she didn't have any reason to tell him, except that she was his friend. A friend would not keep the information to herself. She was stuck. Gina decided that she would go to Dirk's office and tell him what she learned at the gym. Just as she was heading that way, Greta came to tell her Dirk wanted to see her.

"Good." Gina moved over to let Greta pass. "Because I want to see him too."

Entering Dirk's office, Gina smiled. "Good morning, Dirk."

"It's not such a good morning. Why didn't you tell me about the accident a little over a year ago?"

"I am not sure what accident you are referring to. So, I cannot tell you why I didn't tell you."

Dirk turned on her. "This is not the time to be a smart ass. There was an accident with one of the EYE BOTS, and a person was fatally injured."

I have no idea what you are talking about. I came in here to tell you something, Dirk."

"It will have to wait; this is serious. There is a potential lawsuit over an early test EYE BOT. We have the BOT research trial participants sign a waiver in case of harm, but this lawyer has served us with papers indicating negligence and nonfeasance. Who knows about this?"

"I swear to you, I have no idea what you are talking about. When we first tested the BOTS, we got a report that there had been an electrical fire. We requested the BOT back, and tried to investigate, but we were told that the firemen had not found a BOT, and that the damage to most areas of the home was minimal."

"So, you didn't think that was important enough to tell me about? What about Dave, does he know?"

"I presume he does; he is the one who tried to get the BOT back," replied Gina defensively enough that the tone sent Dirk's temperature to a new level of hot.

"Get out of my office, now!" Dirk got on his intercom to Greta and requested that she come to his office immediately.

Greta ran into the office, and when she saw Dirk's face, she knew that something was very wrong. "Dirk?" asked Greta.

"Greta!"

"Dirk, what happened? Why did Gina storm out of here? Should I call Dave to come in to meet with you?" asked Greta timidly.

"We are being sued for something that happened early in testing with one of the BOTS. I had no idea this was going on, or that there had even been an accident.

Yes, get Dave in here. I need some explanations, yesterday!" Greta left the office in search of Dave.

Gina beat a path to Dave's office directly from Dirk's temper tantrum. She flew past the assistant, who didn't even bother to try and stop her.

"Dave, do you remember that BOT that caught on fire due to an electrical shortage? You said it was faulty wiring in the house, and that there was nothing to be concerned about!"

"Yes, Gina, I remember, and that is what I said. Why are you running in here like a crazy woman?"

"Because, Dave, I just got castigated big time for not telling Dirk about a faulty BOT over a year ago, and I did not know he didn't know. He says we are being sued."

At just that moment, Greta arrived, having also run by the assistant without asking if she could go into Dave's office. This time the assistant put his head in the door, and said hesitantly, "Doctor Johnson, there are people here to see you."

"Yes, thank you, Tim, I have it all under control; you can go back to finishing those phone calls I asked you to make."

Tim went back to his desk and contemplated whether he was in the right position.

"Gina, Greta, take deep breaths, and one at a time, tell me what is wrong. I take it that something occurred regarding the BOT that purportedly had an electrical failure over a year ago. There have been no more incidents and I reworked the circuits making sure that it was not the BOT. It was definitely a house circuit that caused the problem."

"Well, you better be prepared to tell Dirk that because he thinks we kept something from him. Apparently, someone died, and we are being blamed for it," said Gina.

Greta added her own take on the situation. "Doctor Keene is angry. He wants you in his office, yesterday, and I am not paraphrasing."

Dave walked past the women on his way to Dirk's office to determine what all the fuss was about.

"Dave, good you're here. Why didn't you tell me someone died because of one of our BOTS over a year ago?"

"Dirk, I didn't tell you because no one died because of one of our BOTS. There was a circuitry fire in a home. I tried to recover the BOT by going to the home and I was told it had been destroyed in the fire. I was told that there was nothing left, by the niece, I believe. That seemed a little fishy at the time; there should have been some titanium left at the very least. I spoke with the fire department chief in the town and he assured me that there was nothing left upon their inspection; they found no robot, even though the damage was mostly smoke. Upon investigation, he believed that the fire was caused by a faulty circuit in the house, not by the BOT as reported by the niece. I was not told that anyone died in the fire."

"Dave, so let me get this straight, you went to a home where one of our EYE BOTS was being used, by someone who is not sighted. You tried to get the BOT back but were told it was destroyed. You were also told that it wasn't the fault of the BOT."

"So far, you are exactly right," Dave calmly replied.

"Then you left and just forgot about it? You did not think it was important to let me know that one of our BOTS burned up? I only own the company! What were you thinking, or were you?"

"Dirk, the fire was not the fault of the BOT. I tried to replace the BOT free of charge to the family. I was told by the niece, or caretaker, or whoever she was, that it would not be necessary. I offered to provide temporary housing, even though the fire chief said it was not our fault. I was just trying to help. No one, at any time mentioned that anyone had died. I swear! I didn't tell you because it seemed of no consequence at the time."

"Well, Dave, it's the 'at the time' that seems to be at issue here. I have a letter from an attorney in Dallas, Texas indicating that we are being sued for the death of a Mrs Betty Carmichael. She was in her seventies and apparently died about a month after the fire according to this letter."

"We cannot be held responsible for a woman's death for a fire that we didn't start."

"Well, apparently someone thinks we can be, and we are."

Gina was in her office, fists clenched and pacing the short length from one side to the other. How dare he treat her like that? All she had done was to move this company forward. She hoped Dave would take care of this. Someone died because of one of their BOTS. This was going to be a nightmare if it got to the news media. She didn't know that any marketing campaign could fix dead.

Dave came in a few minutes later. "Gina, we are going to have to do some investigation into the fire and the supposed death of a Mrs Betty Carmichael. I have the file in my office on the BOT and any information I had collected."

"Dave, not to be insensitive to our situation, but I do not think I should be doing the investigation into a fire and a death. I am a marketing person, in case you forgot. I sell things, not investigate who they killed!"

"Who am I going to get to do this? We can't let this get out to the rest of the organization."

"Dave, I am not sure how to tell you this, but Greta knows. Tell Greta, tell everyone."

"You do have a point there," he said, as a grimace danced across his upper lip. "I guess I will have to go do the investigating." Dave headed back to his office to figure out what to do.

Tim knocked on the door. "May I speak with you, Doctor Johnson?"

"Sure, come on in, Tim."

"Doctor Johnson, I don't know if you remember I am in school for law enforcement and I want to be a detective. I overheard the conversation from next door, because quite frankly Ms Portense is not a very quiet talker, and I am your assistant, so I think I should know what goes on, but never tell anyone. I'd like to investigate for you."

"I don't know, Tim; we are being threatened because allegedly some woman died because of the BOT. It is not true, and I don't know why this is coming up now, except we are a deep pocket. Although not that deep. In any death, the family is always looking for someone to blame. In this case, I guess a higher power wasn't good enough."

"I don't think you should joke about a thing like this, Doctor Johnson. If someone died, and BOTS is being blamed, then it could be profoundly serious for the company."

"Okay, Joe Hardy, you are on the job." Dave reluctantly and deliberately handed a file to Tim. "Start by going through this file. Then have Greta give you copies of the letter from the attorneys. See what it is they are demanding. Do not ask Doctor Keene for the letter if you want to keep your head. Contact the fire chief at the department in Dallas or whatever the name of that suburb is. See if he has any idea why this is coming up now. Once you have all that information, report back to me and we will decide the next steps forward."

"Thank you, Doctor Johnson. I will not let you down. Can I ask a question?"

"Of course you can, Tim."

"Who is Joe Hardy?"

"Ah, I age myself once again. When I was younger, there was a book series called the Hardy Boys. It was a mystery series. I liked it a lot. That, and Encyclopedia Brown. Do you know who Encyclopedia Brown is?"

"No, Doctor Johnson, I don't. But I can look it up on Instagram."

"It's okay, Tim. You will not find it on Instagram. Back to the matters at hand. I know you will not let me down. Leading an investigation has to be more satisfying than having crazy people run past you every day." Dave laughed.

Tim laughed a little too, although he wasn't sure he should.

Twenty-six Victims. Oh My!

Sarah and Kathy met at the Café Italia not far from where Sarah lived. It was an authentic Italian place and had the best eggplant parmigiana. Sarah needed some comfort food. Trying to come up with all the ways to poison someone was making her sad, and that always made her hungry. That was probably her mom's fault, because when she was sad as a child, her mother would cook her favorite foods. Kathy asked for a quiet spot on the patio. She wanted to continue to discuss their investigation. Once they had ordered, the women started to reflect on all the material evidence they had. They now had twenty-six dead bodies. There were three males and all the rest were female, based on the information they had from Dr Canon. The individuals were all over the age of seventy and except for Mr King, none of them were married. All of them lived in either Coconut Grove or Coral Gables and that made Mercy Hospital the closest emergency department when they got ill. All of them were admitted to Mercy Hospital with shortness of breath, symptoms of the flu and complaining of pain in their legs. Beyond that, the rest of the coroner's reports described tissues, and the overall condition of the body. In all the cases, there were no signs of cancer or advanced heart disease.

"That they have very little heart disease is amazing considering their ages," noted Sarah.

"What does that have to do with this?"

"That was just a thought; it has nothing to do with the case, Kathy, sorry."

Kathy continued. "The hospital director said she will have the medical records of all the individuals by tomorrow. There is only Mr King who has positive levels of arsenic in his blood."

The women continued to sort through the data. The first eleven had not been tested and there was no way to go back and test them for heavy metals because they had all been cremated. Most of them did not have influenza even though they had symptoms. The people who died after Mr King had been tested for influenza and for heavy metals but only Mr King and two others seemed to have been poisoned by arsenic. One might have been positive for influenza: Mr Verne.

Sarah scrunched her brow and rubbed her forehead. "You know, there are only four metals in the toxicology test that they do based on what Doctor Canon said. I wonder if there is another metal that might be the cause? I can also try to come up with a test for trumpet flowers and see if any of the victims from here on out have been poisoned with that. It will be difficult though, and I am not even sure it will be possible to detect it because of the way the drug, when derived from the flower, works in the human body. If it is possible, it will take me a few days. I will work with a University of Miami toxicologist I know. He might already have something since the adolescents have found a way to derive a hallucinogenic effect from the plant. I do think that Doctor Canon should test for digoxin levels on the woman that came in today — what is her name — Ruth Morgan, and if there are any more after her. I am afraid there will be more deaths, until we figure this out."

Kathy closed her eyes and lowered her head. "I can't disagree with you. Until we find out why these people are being targeted, in addition to a common place where they have all been other than Mercy Hospital, or a common person, then there will indeed be more deaths."

"Is there anything in the social history from the autopsy reports that will point us in any direction?" asked Sarah.

"I looked a little after I picked up the files from Doctor Canon, but I think we are going to have to spend time going over the reports and the hospital records somewhere like my office where we can spread out, and work undisturbed."

Sarah gritted her teeth and twisted her fingers together into a knot. "I agree with you, we need to be able to make a list of all of the similarities. We might need to start contacting the families."

"Don't get ahead of yourself, Nancy Drew; you will not be contacting families. You are helping me, but you have not been 'deputized' as you put it the other day. You cannot go on official company business with me."

"Oh." As her shoulders drooped, Sarah looked to Kathy with a half-hearted smile. "I have interview skills; I can be a big help."

"Yes, you do, and yes you could. No, you cannot go with me. You can stay behind and dig through the files and see what kind of connections you can make. That seems to be a strength of yours anyway."

"Do you think that there is any chance that someone at the hospital is murdering these people because they are old and alone? I mean, it happens on TV all the time, and there are cases where it has happened in real hospitals."

"That is a good thought too, Sarah, but I don't think that is the case. Unless your digoxin theory holds up and the next few have high levels of it — only then will I think you might be on to something."

I think you should call me Number One, like on Star Trek. You are the captain, and I am your number one. I can 'make it so' when you tell me to."

"No to Star Trek, and really?"

"Okay, call me Nancy Drew." Sarah grinned.

Their meals arrived and the conversation stopped while they savored the food, and the company.

Harold Feels the Heat

Mary and Harold were sitting in the kitchen of their home in Coconut Grove. They lived close to the water. They were able to afford the condo because their home in Euclid, Ohio had gained so much in equity during the fifteen years they lived there. Their home now was a two-bedroom condo, with windows across the back that provided a scenic view of a canal and overlooked the condominium pool. Harold did not want to do lawn-work any more, so this was the perfect setting and compromise. Mary wanted a house on the water, and they could not afford that.

"How is work this week?" asked Mary. "You seem preoccupied."

Harold hung his head. "My boss told me that one of my clients died. He apparently had the flu and was taken to the hospital and died a couple of days later."

"Oh, that is horrible," gasped Mary. "Who is it? Do I know the person?"

"Mary, you know I cannot talk to you about our clients specifically. They are protected under a privacy act."

"I know, but I just want to make sure it isn't someone I know. It's a small world and as big as Miami-

Dade seems to be, there are some days when it seems smaller than Euclid."

"Please, do not bring up Euclid. We left, and it is all behind us. We have moved on to our new life and are settled here."

"Two of the children are still there and six of our grandchildren; we cannot erase it from our past as much as you might like to do that."

"Mary, I don't want to talk about it." Harold stood and headed toward the window slowly.

"Well, Harold, what do you want to talk about? It seems like in the last couple of weeks, you haven't wanted to talk about much. Are you taking your medication?"

He turned and a fist formed out of each hand. "Yes, Mary, I am taking my medication, all of it. Are you taking yours?"

Mary's lips were pursed, and she pointed at Harold. "I only take a blood pressure medicine and I take it every day. I am worried about you; maybe you should go see a counselor, or your doctor. You have not been yourself. Maybe you are working too hard and should cut back on your hours and change shifts to the day shift so we can spend more time together."

Harold reacted to her need, for his own selfish reasons, not for Mary's sake. "I am fine. Do you want me to meet you for lunch tomorrow? I am working late. I can meet you before I go to work."

Harold was sure the invitation would get her off his back. The last thing he wanted was to go on the day shift where he wouldn't see Charleen and would lose all hope of finding alone time with her. Mary would expect him to be home with her, and he already felt like a prisoner in the house. He couldn't stop thinking about his night with Charleen and counting the days until they might be able to steal some more time together. Thoughts of how wet she had been crept into the recesses of his mind and made him yearn for those wet, juicy, tasty lips. He needed more of that, and he was determined to make sure it happened.

"Honey, where are you?" asked Mary, wrinkling her brow. "You asked if I want you to join me for lunch and then you seemed to be lost in thought. A penny for your thoughts?"

"What time should I meet you for lunch? I was just thinking about where we would go, and how nice it will be to take my lovely lady out for a date. We should do that more often. In fact, there are other things we should do more often."

He was feeling the effects of thinking about Charleen and needed to do something to cover his response. He got up and walked around the table to kiss Mary. She turned her face away, and he kissed her cheek. That was not what he had in mind. It took some of the guilt away about Charleen though, because he had tried to do more, and Mary obviously had lost interest in him for anything other than his paycheck and perhaps his company. He felt free to do as he pleased from here on out. To Harold, the act by Mary of turning her cheek gave him permission to go to his paramour.

Harold was a little concerned that one of his clients had died. He was working hard to avoid scandal — well maybe not that hard, considering his feelings for Charleen, but other kinds of scandal that dealt directly with work. What if people started to investigate him or his past? He needed this job, and he needed it now more than ever. Charleen had thrown him a life preserver.

Mary got ready for work and left home for the day. Harold searched through the closet to see if she had brought home any of the chemicals they used at her office. She sometimes did and stored them in the cabinet in the hallway. Harold made ceramic bowls to take his mind from the real world. He used arsenic to whiten his ceramics. It wasn't easy to obtain any more, although go figure, you could still buy it in small amounts in cold medicines where they sold homeopathic concoctions. Mary often helped him out and brought home outdated supplies and marked it destroyed at the office. He didn't find any and made a mental note to ask her if there was a chance of getting more. He felt the need to throw some clay to diffuse his anxiousness.

Harold was having a hard time focusing. He got ready for work early and poured a glass of wine. Then he realized he must drive to work, and so he sat it aside for a cola. He sat on the patio and the warm sun lulled him into deep thought and rest. Charleen approached unexpectedly; she was dressed in a sheer gown, and running toward him. He saw her as the goddess who would rescue him from this place. He reached for her and pulled her to him. He felt his erection and he knew she was ready for him because he felt her sweet, juicy pleasure through her gown. She kissed him and slowly wrapped her hand around his manhood.

"Let it go," whispered Charleen. "Let me feel you cover my body with your juices and free yourself of all your cares."

Oh, he felt so good, he let go and moaned with a sigh and called out for Charleen as he released his tensions into her. He was liberated and relaxed into Charleen's warm, soft, luscious body. Just then the Alexa chimed, telling him it was time to go to work. He shook his head and looked for Charleen. She was not there, only the release that had claimed the front of his pants in the form of a hydra. He recognized the danger but was not going to stop. He got ready for work a second time that day and headed out the door.

Murder, Anyone?

Sarah headed to her class, determined to get her students' thoughts on the murders. But she had to be cautious about the way she approached it. She had already asked them to discuss toxic plants on their class blog. That did not reveal anything that she felt would be useful to the investigation. It was of course useful to the students and they seemed to gain new knowledge from the exercise. They blogged about foxglove and trumpet flowers or the species name *Digitalis purpurea* and *Brugmansia*. These two discussion posts had given her a new thought.

What if someone used nightshade? It is in the same family as the trumpet flower. The *Solanaceae* or nightshade family included *Atropa belladonna*, bell peppers, tomatoes and eggplant. But that did not make sense that a person would have used belladonna berries for poison. There was no report of hallucinations, or paralysis in the records so far. Nightshade was hard to grow too. If an individual were poisoned with nightshade, death would be more instantaneous. Atropine, which was one drug that came from the nightshade family, was used in a variety of hospital settings, and there could be a possibility that someone got atropine from the pharmacy and used it on these individuals. Still, that made no sense, based on the symptoms that they went to the hospital with, but Sarah did not know what happened right before they died. For a person poisoned with nightshade outside the hospital, getting to a hospital in time would be difficult if enough was used. That pretty much eliminated that family of plants.

Sarah looked up, surprised as she almost walked past the door to the classroom. Sarah walked into the classroom and found her students discussing murder.

"Good morning, everyone." She smiled brightly as she entered the classroom.

A few of the students replied with a "Good morning." A few more just gave her a nod, and a couple of them were more engrossed in the conversation and did not appear to have time for politeness.

"I want to commend you on your discussion board posts. For the most part they are written well, and thorough, and thoughtful. Just what I expect from a group of PhD students. What were all of you so intently discussing as I entered? I thought I heard the word murder?"

"We were discussing the fact that you asked us to write about poisonous plants. Some of us went on the internet to get ideas. It is scary how many wives poison their husbands with a variety of toxic substances. What is even scarier are the cases where a health care worker felt that they were helping people by killing them because they were going to die anyway. On TV it's always the pharmacist who is the murderer." Gary gave a low deep villainous laugh as he finished.

The whole class cracked up laughing. Presumably because they all knew that Sarah's first degree was in pharmacy and that she kept her license current in Florida.

Taylor, who did not say much usually, looked seriously at Sarah. "We wondered who you are planning on killing, and if it's one of us."

The only one who did not seem to find the conversation funny was Charleen and she was not saying much. Sarah wondered why.

"Well, I am not planning a murder. In case you do not know, it's against the law, wise asses. I am writing a novel about murder and I'll admit it, I need some help figuring out how the murderer will do it."

Jordan spoke up. "Doctor Sandling, you expect us to believe that? You already know all this stuff; you don't need us to help you. What's really going on?"

"Jordan, this is a formal course and I have a responsibility as your faculty member to prepare you to be a pharmacognosist. There are multiple ways to do that; getting you to understand and have the skills to determine when a plant will be beneficial and when it will be poisonous is part of that. I take my position as your faculty member very seriously."

"Doctor Sandling, how do you determine if someone has been poisoned by a plant or something else?"

"That, Charleen, is a great question. There are not a lot of tests for specific plants. The toxicologist or the medical examiner will have to rely on the symptoms that are reported to be present prior to the individual getting sick and or dying. It is a little out of our specialty to investigate crimes. Back to your question though — the short answer is the forensic examiner will look for clues in tissues, and body organs, and will put that together with evidence which can include meals and other social history things like smoking, family or workplace. That is about as much as I know about forensic medicine. You'll have to watch 'Law and Disorder' to get the rest of your education in that area."

The class laughed. At least she had reduced the tension that had suddenly been brought on by Charleen's question.

"All kidding aside, Doctor Sandling," asked Charleen, "do you think that using a medicinal plant as poison is a crime that a person could get away with if they wanted to?"

"I hope not, Charleen. I hope the system will work and they will be caught and brought to justice."

Sarah quietly put away her course notes as she wondered where all these questions were coming from. Sarah turned her attention back to the students.

"Class, this has been a remarkably interesting discussion for me, but I am not sure you are learning what I planned for you. Did anyone read the chapters in Buss and Butler that were assigned for today? Anyone want to discuss the new technologies that will aid us in improving the natural product pipeline for drugs?" Sarah waited and observed the faces of her students. "So, that is a no, then." Sarah crossed her arms and made a face to express her feelings.

Gary spoke up. "I read it, but I don't want to discuss it. Tell us more about murder."

Charleen raised her hand. "I read the whole book. I want to work in drug discovery. Why did natural products fall out of favor? I know what the book says about time, money, and technology, but that all sounds like an excuse. You went to Peru and studied medicinal plants. Why aren't we using some of those plants and developing them as drugs? You said there was a sap from a tree that worked like a living band-aid."

"That is true, Charleen. Much of the problem in the past that limited drug discovery really was time, money, and the amount of effort it took to extract products like that natural band-aid from the sap in the tree. In addition, we really should not be cutting down the rainforest. It is important to find other ways. I expect that you will all be prepared to discuss those chapters the next time we meet. I will see you in lab tomorrow. Have a good afternoon."

Sarah headed back to her office to continue thinking about the murders. She found it interesting that Charleen asked such insightful questions. Why was Charleen asking those questions? It seemed sinister to be asking if she thought a person could get away with murder if they used a medicinal plant. They had already looked on the internet and seen how many times people have not gotten away with it. What you do not see is how many times people have been able to commit murder and not get caught. She wondered if she and Kathy were going to be able to find the answers that were necessary for the current case. What would happen if they didn't?

A shudder ran the length of her torso and the hair rose on her arms as she thought about it. More people would die. Just then her phone buzzed because she had forgotten to take it off silent. Sarah jumped at the sensation, realizing she had been lost in thought.

Sarah looked down at her phone and it was her mother calling. She had not talked to her in a while and supposed she should pick up and see what she wanted.

"Hello, Mom, how are you?"

"Honey, I am fine, but I am worried about you. I have not heard from you. I haven't seen Chloe and I don't know what you are eating these days."

"Mom, really, you don't know what I am eating? I have been gone from home for quite a few years. Why are you calling?"

"Well, it's complicated. I do not really know who else to ask. I know that you don't practice pharmacy any more, but I am hoping you might know the answer to this question."

"Okay, Mom, ask away."

"Well, I actually have some sad news first. Do you remember my friend Ruth Morgan?"

"Mom, what did you just say?"

"I said do you remember my friend Ruth Morgan?"

Sarah thought to herself, how many Ruth Morgans can there be? Looking at the phone in surprise, Sarah replied, "No, Mom, I don't really remember her; does she play canasta with you?"

"Yes, and she goes to church with me as well. I am calling because she got a flu shot about two weeks ago. I was just informed by Gladys that she died. I am wondering if the flu shot killed her. There, I've said it."

"Mom, number one, NO, and I emphasize, NO, the flu shot did not kill her."

"How do you know? You don't know anything about her!"

"You'd be surprised what I know about, Mom. I know for sure vaccines do not kill people; they keep them from dying from the flu and other diseases."

"Well, Gladys said that Ruth got the flu shot and then she got flu symptoms and went to the hospital. Now she is dead, she is dead. Am I going to die?" asked her mother who sounded as if she was getting rather hysterical on the other end of the phone.

"Mom, Mom, listen to me, you are not going to die from the flu shot or the flu."

Although with all the other cases, and her mom being seventy-five, Sarah wasn't sure how she could guarantee that. This was now hitting a little too close to home.

"Mom, I am headed home to get Chloe and we will come over for dinner. I want to hear more about your friend Ruth."

Putting Out Fires

Shaking his head and dropping it into his hands, Tim sat at his desk. He was getting nowhere on the investigation. This was his chance to prove that he was valuable to Dr Johnson, and he was not making particularly good progress. He called the Baronsky and Hart law offices and was told that if Dr Keene received their letter, and apparently, he must have since he had his assistant calling, then there was nothing to do but wait to hear from their office further. While he rummaged through papers on his desk, his feelings were expressed by the heavy handedness of the activity.

There must be something more he could do with the law office. This had to be about money. Wouldn't a client want to settle with BOTS Inc. and get the money and not go to court? Surely Dr Keene would settle, but Dr Johnson seemed to believe that it was not a faulty EYE BOT. What were the options? He would try another avenue to get the information he needed. Dr Johnson had mentioned the fire chief.

Picking up the phone, Tim called Plano Fire Station 4. Tim waited patiently through the recording before he could leave a message for the chief. He hoped they had records of the fire or would remember Mrs Betty

Carmichael or both. Dr Johnson hurried through the office doors and asked if Tim had been able to get any information on the fire, or Mrs Carmichael.

"Not yet. I just put in a call to the fire station. The law offices won't share any information with me; they said to wait until we get another letter from them."

"Oh, Dirk isn't going to like that. We need to do some more detective work. Keep digging, Tim, as if your life depends on it."

"I hope that is not the case, sir, or my job."

"It isn't, Tim, but we need to proceed as if it is, understood?"

"Yes, sir, I do."

Gina followed right behind Dave. She rushed through the door on his heels and looked at Tim. "I'm going in; are you going to stop me?"

"Absolutely not, Ms Portense, feel free to go right on in." Smiling, he thought, I know how to handle her. It has only taken two years, four months and one day. Let Dr Johnson deal with her.

"What did you find out, Dave? Did you call the family? Did you call the lawyer? Did you do anything, or are you just going to let this slide like you did before?"

"Gina, you have got to calm down about this. Everything is going to be okay."

Gina's voice raised two pitches higher as she squeaked, "Calm down, calm down — how am I supposed to do that? There is someone out there trying to sue us, we don't know who died or why and I cannot continue to market a product that catches on fire and cannot do math!"

"We probably do know who died. Her name is Betty Carmichael; at least that is what I am presuming, since she was leasing the EYE BOT. She was an old woman. She probably died after the fire for some other reason and the family is just looking for someone to blame. They always are. We are a good target for an attorney."

"When you went to see this Betty person, did you talk to her?"

"No, I talked to her niece. She seemed intelligent and told me that her aunt was old and senile and had lost her husband and that it would all work out, not to worry."

"She said not to worry, and you accepted that?" Gina turned an interesting shade of red as the conversation continued.

"Yes, I did."

"Well, you must have been born yesterday because any time a woman says 'don't worry', there is always something to worry about. Just for future reference!"

"Wow, is there any way for me to talk you off this ledge you have climbed out onto, Gina?"

"Well, maybe a nice dinner and some wine, if you are asking."

Dave asked determinedly, already knowing the answer was yes, "And will it stop at a nice dinner and wine?"

"Yes, it will. We're friends and I am sorry if I am a little upset over this, but I want the company to be successful and I just think you don't seem to be as concerned as you should be."

Sadly, hanging his head, he accepted rejection again. He was buoyed by the rules of no dating each other per Dirk's direction and was hoping that Gina was just abiding by them. "That's because there is nothing to be concerned about. I'll pick you up at your place tonight and we'll go chill somewhere with dinner and a glass of wine."

Gina thanked him and left the office. As she passed Tim, she growled, "What are you looking at?"

Tim smiled.

Dirk was always in the office early and today was no different. There was so much to think about and it all of it did not have to do with business. The issue of the exploding EYE BOT was a concern. Feeling that Dave did what he could at the time, Dirk shrugged and took a seat at the desk. If this family of Betty Carmichael was going to push the issue, he had attorneys that would deal with it. Dirk rubbed his forehead and realized the company attorneys needed to be cautious. He did not want to create a public relations nightmare for Gina. He did not know if she could handle it. He probably needed to apologize to her for his behavior the other day. She had caught him at a bad time, and he did not handle it well. He wondered if she was in her office.

Dirk stood up to go see Gina and he realized she had also said she had something else to tell him, and he had not listened to her. I guess I better go find her, he thought.

He walked over to her office and she wasn't in. Grabbing a pen from her desk, he left her a note. 'Come see me when you get a chance, I owe you an apology. Dirk.'

On second thoughts, he picked up that note, threw it in the trash and wrote, 'I am an asshole, come see me please, when you can.'

He headed back to his office, and on the way to there was thinking about how he treated Greta. What did she mean by those comments on the personal assistant BOT? He needed to talk to her too.

It seemed like a lot of apologizing and he was usually more collected than he had been the last few days. It was not just the threat of a lawsuit. It was that girl! She had gotten under his skin and he could not do a thing about it. Maybe he needed a massage. It had been a long time since he'd had one, and there were more than a few knots that needed to be worked out.

Dirk arrived back at the office, and asked Greta to join him. He offered her a seat in the chairs in front of his desk and he took the one next to her.

"Greta, I am sorry. I was harsh the other day with both you and with Gina. I walked over to her office to apologize and she was not there. I was disrespectful to both of you, and I apologize."

Greta was not sure what to say. She sat upright in her chair. She knew that Dirk was under a lot of pressure, but she was feeling more used than appreciated lately. The idea of a personal assistant BOT was infuriating because what would be next, BOTs that will pee for you? Greta laughed at the thought and then addressed Dirk.

"Dirk, thank you for apologizing. I understand you are under a lot of pressure. I have known you a long time. What is really going on? You haven't been this agitated since you were left at the altar."

"Greta, do you have to keep bringing that up? I am over it. I am glad she left me. Now, you seemed a little offended by the idea of a personal assistant BOT. Couldn't you use a robot to help you accomplish your mundane repetitive tasks during the day, so you can do other work?"

"Perhaps when you put it that way. It seems to me, though, if you create a personal assistant BOT then you will not need people like me. For many years, there have been predictions that robots will take over all human functions, well except for maybe a few, but I am not even sure they won't be able to do that better than humans. Excuse my brevity." Her cheeks turned bright red and Greta slid a little lower in her chair.

"No excusing needed. You are right; people are afraid that the robot and artificial intelligence will replace humans. The people saying that robots will replace humans forget that robots can only do what the humans program them to do. They are just tools, so to speak. The world will use robots and artificial intelligence to do more tasks. Humans work far too many hours, and we are on the Earth for such a short time. Won't it be better to have more free time to think, and play and spend less time doing mundane things? That is my vision for the world."

"Dirk, I hope you are right. Now, you avoided my question. What is bothering you?"

"Greta, you are more like my mom, well, than my mom, so I'll tell you. I ran into a woman a while ago, and I cannot get her out of my mind. The problem is, I don't know her name, I don't know where she lives, and I want to see her again."

Greta responded with an, "Ahhhh," and a light touch on Dirk's forearm. "You will figure it out. You are a smart man. I need to get back to work before I am replaced by a personal BOT." Greta laughed on her way out of the door. She shut it behind her and let Dirk alone with his thoughts.

Dinner with the Parents

Sarah arrived at her mother's house in Kendall with Chloe, who led the way to the front door. Sarah's mother Jean stepped out to greet them and Chloe firmly planted a wet kiss on her face. "Oh, hello my sweet Chloe, thank you for taking such good care of my baby Sarah. I know you protect her and keep her safe. When I talk to you, girl, what do you hear? Is it blah, blah, blah, or do you really understand me?" She laughed because she knew this dog was smart enough to save her daughter's life if necessary, so she must know more than blah, blah, blah.

"Hi. Mom, now you kiss her before me. I know where those lips have been! Chloe's, not yours. Just give me a hug." Sarah laughed as she threw her arms around her mother's neck and squeezed her tight. "I love you, Mom."

"Well, honey, I am not sure what I did to deserve that, but thank you, and I love you too. Come inside and eat."

"Mom, always with the eating. I am trying to lose weight. Chloe and I walk every day."

"You're too thin already," replied her mom in that way that only an Italian mother can.

Sarah laughed, thinking, we aren't even Italian, we're from Ireland; how can she possibly sound like an Italian grandma?

She let it go and moved inside the house to kiss her father. Sarah really wanted to get the information about Ruth Morgan, but she was afraid that eating would be required before any information would be shared. But she tried.

"Mom, I am so sorry to hear about your friend Ruth. What happened?"

"Oh, honey, I am so sad. But we should eat first and then I can tell you all about it. I just don't want to ruin your appetite."

Sarah gave up and grabbed a plate of food because she recognized the futility of trying to get out of eating when her mother had prepared her favorites.

After the kitchen and dishes were cleaned up, Jean said, "We should sit in the dining room and have some wine and I'll tell you all about poor Ruth. What kind of wine, darling?"

"No wine! Let's go sit in the living room and you will tell me all about it. What happened?"

"Well, you know Ruth was in particularly good health. She was a highly active person as well. She walked until about a couple of months ago. She walked well over a mile a day. She taught Sunday school and was always at the canasta parties on our regular Tuesdays."

Sarah motioned with her hands and urged her mother to go on with the story. "You asked me about the flu vaccine. When did she get that? What makes you think she died from that? You seemed very convinced on the phone."

"Well, I don't know exactly when she got the vaccine. She started having some pain in her legs a while ago. I do not remember how long that was. She decided it was time to see her physician. She thought maybe she had a blood clot or something awful. I think it was about that time that the doctor also told her to get the flu shot since she was active and around crowds of people and since, you know, she was older. It is hard for me to say old, since she is, or was, just a few years older than I am. I'm not afraid to die, but I don't want it to happen any time soon."

"Mom, you are healthy; let's hope that you do have a long time here, but life is short, and precious as we both know. You are getting off track. Tell me more about Ruth."

"There really isn't much to tell; she doesn't have any family to speak of. Her husband has been dead for many years. They never got to have any children. She was an only child. She lived here in Florida for most of her life. That is really all I know about her, except that she was a dreadful canasta player. Everyone would quietly try not to be her partner because if you were you knew you would be losing your pennies that night."

"Thanks, Mom, that's all very interesting and I am sad, but what about her having the flu?"

"Oh, that, well I thought you weren't supposed to get the flu if you had a flu shot."

"You only get the flu after you have had the flu shot if it's a different kind of flu than what the makers put in the flu vaccine that year."

"You mean there are different kinds of flu?"

"Yes, Mom, you know that we have talked about it before. This year the flu shot seems to be highly effective, so I find it hard to believe Ruth died of the flu. Did this come on suddenly?"

"Why are you asking so many questions? You seem overly interested."

Sarah decided she was going to have to be a little less overt about her questioning in order not to have to spill the beans to her mom. She knew that the people who died had flu symptoms and not much family, so those pieces certainly coincided with every detail they had so far been able to piece together.

"Oh, Mom, I am just interested since she is, or was, your friend and I know you are sad. What other kind of activities did Ruth do? Did she have a special friend?"

"You mean a man?"

"Well, or woman, either one."

"No, she was alone most of the time; she would say that she was lonely. I know she liked to go to the spa and whatever it is you do in those places."

"Mom, you make it sound dirty. It is relaxing and fun. Have you ever gone to a spa? They do manicures, and pedicures, you can get a facial, or a massage, or seaweed wrap."

"Stop right there. Who on earth wants seaweed wrapped around them? I spent years when we snorkeled trying to stay out of the seaweed!"

"Mom, not the same concept. So, she went to the spa. Did she do that last week?"

"Humm, I don't know. I know she had a regular appointment somewhere and it wasn't for her hair."

"Mom, did you ever play cards at her place?" asked Sarah, trying to probe without being too suspicious.

"Well, yes we did, come to think of it. She lived in an apartment complex for seniors. I wonder who is taking care of that place now, as I don't know that there is anyone to do that for her."

"If you can find out from your friends who might be doing that, then I will be happy to help you."

"I will see what needs to be done, thank you, honey."

"Not a problem, Mom. Chloe, we need to get going."

"Woof." Chloe appeared from her napping spot and ran to the front door. Sarah kissed her dad good night and hugged her mother as she headed for the door herself.

"Good night, Sarah; be careful driving home. I love you."

Unlocking the car, Sarah climbed in and got Chloe into the passenger seat. She pulled out her phone to text Kathy.

Sarah: Hey, I just had dinner with mom. She knew the last lady that died. She did not have any family. Maybe if we find out where she lived, we could see if she has anything in her apartment that will help us. Can we do that?
Kathy: Driving, but yes, we can do that.

Kathy had been to Mercy to pick up the records of the twenty-six people who had died. The hospital director seemed very alarmed, which was appropriate. It would have been odd if she had not been concerned that she might have a murderer among her staff. Kathy had also spoken to the Miami-Dade prosecutor to ensure that when she needed the search warrants, she could get them expeditiously without too much problem. One never knew about the prosecutor; his penchant for drinking and gambling was a rumor that was likely true, but he kept being re-elected. Go figure, anything was possible in South Florida. That was the intrigue when living in Miami-Dade County; there were just some crazy crimes, committed by very odd criminals. The Miami Herald columnist Clay Hasson had written about many of them. He was a favorite author of Kathy's.

This was like a Clay Hasson crime. That man had a dry, dark sense of humor. All she was missing in this case was the crazy ex-governor. The criminal here would do something stupid. She knew it. Arriving at the building, Kathy headed to her office and dropped the files on her desk before she texted Sarah.

Kathy: I am at the office do you want to come over and start going through some of the records tonight?

Sarah: I'll head over as soon as I drop Chloe off,

Kathy: Bring her, we are here all alone tonight, it will be good to have a guard dog.

Sarah arrived at the office with Chloe and a dog bone to keep her occupied while she and Kathy worked, because otherwise Sarah was afraid Chloe would get into mischief. Puppies took so much time, but Chloe was turning into a great dog. They went up the elevator to Kathy's offices and knocked on the thick glass doors that did not appear to be locked but would not budge when Sarah pulled the handle.

Sarah: We're here.

Kathy came to the door and let them in. Sarah commented on the way back to the workspace, "I see that there is no signage, and your offices are not listed in the directory downstairs."

"Yes, that is correct," Kathy grinned. "So, you still don't know what agency I work for and it will stay that way."

"I don't care any more. I am glad you trust me enough to help you; I am having fun."

"I have all the files from the coroner, and all the files from the hospital. Let's match names, and then split them up and start looking through the files to see if there is anything that we can do to link these people other than they had flu symptoms and died in the same hospital."

Frustrations Get the Best of Dirk

"Greta, will you make me an appointment for a massage please. I am feeling a little tense. Just make it at one of those MassageMe places. I want a male."

It was not really a big corporate office and if it were not for the white noise machines, everyone would be able to hear all the conversations; sometimes they could anyway. That was how small the place was. That was also how Greta knew everything. In addition, she ate lunch with every assistant in the place at least once a month and they had monthly meetings. If it weren't so aggravating it would be one of the things Dirk appreciated most about her.

"Yes, boss, I think that's a good idea," replied Greta. "I'll get right on it."

Dirk was pondering all the things that had happened during the week. The letter from the attorney was lying on the desk in front of him. He read it again. He thought about his plans for the company and what a lawsuit would mean. He was about to put the EYE BOTS into mass production. They were excellent for the blind, but there were so many more places where they could be relevant. Then he remembered his conversation with Gina about math. He had been distracted. What was it she had said? Did she say they couldn't do math? He thought they had tested that.

Dirk contemplated what it meant for his company if a BOT that was supposed to be able to receive bills, calculate the amount to be paid, calculate checking account balances, write an electronic check and send it to the appropriate place was not working correctly because the math algorithm was incorrect. That couldn't be good. He wondered what Dave was doing about this.

Dirk wandered over to Dave's office. "Tim, is Dave in and available?"

Tim looked up in shock; no one ever asked him that question. He was not sure how to answer.

"Just a minute, Doctor Keene, I will check. Thank you for asking."

Tim got up and went to the door of Dave's office. Dave waved him in.

"Doctor Keene is here to see you."

"Send him in."

Tim returned to the outer office and indicated to Dirk with a wave that he should go on in.

"Well, well, it's been a busy week. What can I do for you, my friend?" asked Dave.

"Dave, I am sorry about the other day if I was a little over the top with you and Gina."

"Is that what you call it? I'd call it being a CEO who got caught off guard, taking it out on his colleagues, some of us who are friends, and who is now eating crow. Although that expression might age me a bit. What is it the youngsters say, groveling?"

"Ow, that hurts. But I guess I earned it. I'm here about the math and the lawsuit. I am just wondering what is going on?"

"Dirk, the BOTS failed math 101. We have had complaints from every one of the people who has one that a bill was either paid and drained their bank account because it didn't add correctly, or a bill wasn't paid because it didn't subtract correctly and didn't recognize that their account had enough money to pay the bill. That is the long and the short of it, so to speak. It would be funny if it wasn't so serious. I tested a couple. I think it's in the backend algorithm. Initially, when testing, we had a bit of a problem, but I thought it was worked out. I didn't hear anything in the first eight months the BOTS were out, and so I thought it was fixed. It seems to have all gone haywire this last week. The best I can tell, when we sent an upgrade a few days ago, someone put an old algorithm back in to the upgrade. Yesterday we sent out messages to everyone to put the BOT to sleep for twelve hours so we could send a new software update. I worked with engineering and we put the right algorithm back into the program and updated every one of the BOTS. The old algorithm will no longer be accessible from anywhere but my computer. I believe that will be the fix."

"Thank you, Dave, for the explanation and for so quickly finding the problem and correcting the issue. I am glad you have my back."

"I always will. I also offered to pay overage charges and late fees for all of the customers. Tim made personal phone calls to each one and got information to plan for payment directly to accounts. I knew that is what you would want me to do."

"Perhaps, but it's why I have you. Thank you for getting ahead of a marketing problem. What about the lawsuit?"

"That is a little harder to fix, I am afraid. Tim and I are working on that. He got stalled when he called the law offices. It seems they want to go to court. That seems unreasonable, and I can't imagine why. He contacted the fire chief in Plano where it happened and is hoping to get a call back today. We may make a trip out there."

"Do what you have to do. I will have the attorneys make a call to the law offices; it was probably some lackey who knew she had a lackey on the other end and was saying what they told her to. When an attorney calls, they know we are paying attention," said Dirk as he turned to walk out of the office. "Good work, Dave, thank you." On the way past Tim, Dirk leaned over to him. "Good work, Tim, thank you." Tim almost dropped his tablet on the floor.

Dirk stopped by the attorney's office since it was on the way back to his. The attorney, Pat, looked up from her desk as Dirk knocked on the door trim. She motioned for him to come in and to have a seat as she finished a phone call. He looked around the office; she had degrees from all the right places. He counted on her for all the company legal business, from stock issuance to lawsuits it now seemed.

"Dirk, I have been waiting for you to come see me. I heard a couple of days ago that there may be a lawsuit over one of the EYE BOTS. I am surprised it has taken you this long to come by. You must not be that worried?"

"In truth it has taken me a little while to pull it together. I was angry the first day I got the letter and took it out on people that did not deserve it. I decided that I did not want to put you on that list. Although, you wouldn't have known about it and not told me."

"Umm, well... Dave came to talk to me last summer when the BOT was blamed for the fire. So, I am as much at fault for not telling you as Gina or Dave. I sent a letter to the family and offered in the letter as Dave had done verbally to provide some temporary housing even though the company was not responsible for the fire."

"You what!" Dirk flew out of his chair. "How could you possibly set us up like that? Did you even think about talking to me? Am I still the CEO? It is one thing for Dave to make a verbal offer and be turned down, but you sent them a letter almost saying well we don't think we are guilty but just in case, we'll put you up somewhere temporarily to assuage our guilt! What were you thinking? It is not like you left law school at," and here Dirk pointed to the diploma on the wall, "Harvard yesterday. This is worse than Dave and Gina not telling me. I am leaving before I say something that I will regret. Don't call me; I'll call you."

Gina was on her way again to tell Dirk about finding Sarah, since she didn't get a chance the last time, and had been staying out of his way. She heard the last little bit of the conversation with Pat, because everyone in the office heard it. Gina leaned her head into Pat's office to see how she was. Pat was sitting at the desk looking like she did not know whether to scream or pack up and leave.

"I got that the other day," Gina said, "but I think you might have just gotten worse. He has been edgy for a while, way worse than after, well you know the thing."

"Yeah, I know the thing. It's like in Harry Potter when no one will say Voldemort and they say he who must not be named instead. I think I just had a run in with he who must not be named."

"On a good note, it seems that the BOTS math problem has been solved with a program update. Did Dave talk to you about reimbursing anyone who had charges and having them sign a form that they won't request anything else or sue us?"

"No, he didn't; please tell me that no letters have been sent?"

"I can't tell you that. I guess you'll be on your way to Dave's office now. Have a good day."

Gina turned to go to her office because there was no way she was going to see Dirk in the mood he was in now. She knew the longer she waited to tell him that she risked him being upset at her rather than happy that she found his dream girl. She decided to take her chances, then she had an epiphany. Gina went back to her office and sent a text to China.

Gina: Do you want to go work out at the gym?

Gina's phone chirped.

China: Not today see you at six PM tomorrow.

Now that the gym appointment was set, Gina wondered if she should text Sarah and ask her to meet her there for some important information. Maybe that would get her out of telling Dirk about Sarah if it was up to Sarah to find him. She sent a text to Sarah.

Unknown: You don't know me, but I have information you may want. Meet me at Star Fitness at six PM tomorrow evening.

Lunch and Anticipation

Harold met Mary for lunch. He picked her up from the lab and took her to the El Rey De Las Fritas on Calle Ocho in Little Havana. They both liked the Cuban sandwich and fries, plus the place was original and cheap. Sometimes those were the best. In Miami, there were many dives and some of the food was excellent. However, eating at some of the dive establishments might give one hepatitis. It was a risk that everyone who lived or ate in the county understood.

Harold placed their order at the counter and followed Mary to a table in the back.

"Harold, thank you for getting me from work today. I feel like we haven't been communicating well for a few weeks."

This was exactly the kind of conversation Harold did not want to have with Mary. He wondered why they couldn't just come to lunch and have a nice meal without all kinds of drama.

"Mary, we have both been terribly busy. It is difficult when we work on different shifts to see each other often."

Here was where Harold had prepared an answer before Mary even asked him to change shifts again.

"I make much better tips in the afternoon and evening. During the day it is just housewives and college kids who get massages. Sometimes I do not even get a tip. You know we depend on the extra for the movies and eating out."

"Well, I just feel like we don't get to do those things as much now."

"I promise you a vacation with the extra money from the tips, how's that?"

"That is a wonderful idea, Harold. You are so thoughtful. I don't know what I would do without you."

Harold had a moment of guilt, but it was replaced quickly with desire as thoughts of Charleen crept into his mind.

"Changing the subject, Mary, I was going to make some pottery yesterday and I looked for some of the special sauce that I put in. You know what I am talking about. The powder you bring home sometimes that makes the clay white."

Catching on to what Harold was talking about, Mary began to nod her head. Since they were in a public place, Mary presumed he didn't want to implicate himself in an arsenic scheme.

"Oh, I did not realize that you were all out. What happened to that big bottle that I brought home recently?"

"I used it all in the last batch of clay I made. Will you be able to bring more home?"

"I will check the supplies and see what I am able to do. It may take me a day or two."

"Thank you, Mary. You know it contributes to reducing my stress."

He thought to himself that with Charleen in the picture he probably didn't have to make that much pottery, but better to have the arsenic handy, just in case. When their meal was complete, it was time to take Mary back to the office and for Harold to head to work. He dropped Mary off and she kissed him on the cheek.

"Don't wait up for me," he said. "I have clients until close."

He pointed the car in the direction of MassageMe and began to whistle. He smiled as he realized it was the first time in a long time that he had whistled on his way to work.

Harold arrived at the MassageMe and headed in to prepare for the first client of the day. He stopped by the office where Corina, his boss, sat to complete the office paperwork.

"Hi, Corina, how is your day? It is a lovely day today, isn't it?"

Corina looked up and smiled and nodded. Sometimes she did not understand Harold because he spoke so rapidly. So, she had taken to just smiling and nodding unless there was something she needed to explain to him. The other night when it was reported that his client had died, she had to talk to him. Today she had gotten a call that another client had died.

Ay, dios mio, she thought to herself. How are there two dead people?

She cancelled the standing appointment in the computer for Ruth Morgan and went back to her work, with a wave to Harold as he was not the massage therapist for Ruth Morgan.

Harold headed to the back of the offices where the staff room was located. He checked the schedule and saw that Charleen would be in today at five. His schedule was full until then and so he was sure that he would be able to keep himself distracted until she got to the office. He looked at the rest of the schedule and saw that once again they were the only two therapists left at the end of the day. This is working out nicely, he thought.

He recognized that feeling of need rising as he pondered the scene that could take place later. He had not told Charleen about his dream, and he did not intend to. It provided him with ideas and his anticipation gave way to concern when he thought that perhaps she might not reciprocate his feelings. But she had said she wanted to be with him again, so surely, she must. His first client got a two-hour massage, so he filled his water bottle, and went to the room to make sure everything was prepared including the massage cream. MassageMe provided the therapists with cream, but he liked to use his own brand and to put some additives in so that the skin absorbed the oils better. He told his clients about using the special lotion so that they felt they were getting extra special treatment from him. Some clients preferred the MassageMe brand and so he always told them that is what he used, even though he always used the one he mixed himself. He kept a supply of gloves in his drawer for use during massages; he checked to make sure there were enough available for the work today. He had psoriasis and didn't want the clients to feel the rough skin on his hands.

Charleen arrived at the office a half an hour early to get ready for her shift. She had been thinking about Harold all week. She got excited and flushed as she remembered how incredible he had made her feel. She had never had an orgasm that rocked her whole body like the one he gave her. In fact, she could only remember ever having one other orgasm in her life and then she wasn't sure what it was, so it might not count. Her girlfriends said she needed to get a vibrator because it could make all the difference in your daily 'attitude of gratitude'. She wasn't so sure about that — her mother caught her playing with herself once when she was in high school and her mother spanked her and grounded her for a week and told her it was a sin. That had taken all the fun out of it for Charleen; she never did that again. She had a few boyfriends when she was in college, but they would suck her tits and push her dress up, fumbling around down there and it was over almost before it began. She lived with a couple of different men over the years and they would tell her to come so they could 'get it over with'. She went online, after that, and watched a YouTube video to learn how to fake an orgasm. It seemed to make them happy, but sex had never been a high point in life for her. She did not really understand why some of her girlfriends liked it so much. One of her friends, Jenna, had multiple vibrators, and multiple boyfriends. Jenna said it gave her variety. Jenna compared it to buying several flavors of ice cream and enjoying each one because it had a different texture and taste.

Charleen was thinking that everything was changing now that Harold had made love to her. He cared about her. He caressed her and made her feel like she was going to shatter and then it got even bigger until she lost all sense of being and just let go. Thinking about it now was making her wet. She had been aroused more than once in the last week thinking about him and the things he had done to her with that massager. She thought maybe she should get a few different toys to play with when they were together. She had never done that before either. She walked through the door of a whole new world when she said yes to Harold. She had not seen him since. She wondered if it would be awkward when she did. She looked at the schedule and saw that they were the only two closing tonight. Hope sprang eternal.

Harold caught Charleen between clients at seven o'clock. There were other people in the hall and so he downplayed the greeting because no one could know what he and Charleen were doing.

"Hello, Charleen, I hope you had a good week. Did you do anything interesting?"

Charleen just looked at him, wondering how he could be so calm — or was it just a one-night thing?

"Hi, yourself. I cleaned house, and went grocery shopping, so no I would not say I did anything interesting. You?"

Harold thought to himself that he had blown it. She did not want him, but then again, he did not want her to fall all over him right now with others in the hall.

"Maybe you want to have a drink later?" he asked, hoping that would clue her in to his continued interest and caring.

"Sure."

"I have to get to my next client. I'll see you after."

Harold met his next client and took them into the room. He found out what he wanted for a massage and then exited while he got ready. Harold hoped to catch Charleen, but she was already in a room. He would have to wait. Harold finished the next massage and checked his client out at the front desk. Harold was sure that fortune was smiling upon them. The girl that came in tonight to take care of the front desk in place of Tracy got ill and had to go home. He decided against calling anyone else to come in since there was only one more client for Charleen and one more for him. The fewer people around the office the better as far as he was concerned. He knew the front desk routine because, sadly, this wasn't the first time he had had to take care of it. The difference was this time, he felt happy rather than being put upon. He thought to himself, the joys of life really were all about perspective. The next two clients came in; he checked them in and completed the night's transactions so that there was nothing to hold him up later.

He alerted Charleen that her next client was waiting up front using the staff room buzzer. Then he walked back and met her in the hallway.

"Charleen, I want you and I want to kiss you and hold you, and maybe do a few other things," he whispered in her ear as he brushed too closely to her on the way to give the next client their massage.

That stopped Charleen in her tracks. The brush against her set her whole being on fire. How was she going to make it through this next hour?

Finally, the end of an hour arrived. For both Harold and Charleen it felt like an eternity. Harold walked the clients out and locked the front door. He practically ran back to Charleen. He slowed his walk because the rising excitement he was feeling had made a rapid pace slightly awkward. Charleen was standing in the hall looking radiant.

"Charleen, I didn't see you all week and I wondered whether, or if, or how you felt about our last time. It is difficult for me to get away other than to be here with you. But trust me, I want you."

"Harold, stop, I want you. I have been anticipating the moments all week thinking about the next time I would get to see you, and it's now, and I don't want to waste a moment talking. Take me someplace and let me make you happier than you have ever been."

"Darling, I don't know if it's healthy for me to get much happier than I already am," he whispered into her ear as he took a handful of her hair and inhaled, relaxing to the scent of the ocean that was lingering. Harold then took her face in his hands and he kissed her until the lips of her mouth were swollen and more beautiful than ever in his opinion. He filled her mouth with his tongue and tasted the eagerness there as Charleen was already moaning a soft low sound that was music to his ears. He placed his hand on her breast and felt the budding of her nipple through the uniform.

"It's time for this to go, and for us to get into a more comfortable place and position" he moaned through the kisses.

Harold slowly directed Charleen while kissing her into the room that he had prepared earlier.

Charleen started to wiggle out of her scrubs and reached to take off her bra.

"Wait," Harold grabbed her hands. "This is one of my favorite things to do. There are a few others but releasing those soft round melons from their prison and watching them fall into my hands gives me so much pleasure."

Charleen obliged; meanwhile she started to untie the scrubs around his waist so that she could get to his family jewels. No one had ever spoken to Charleen like that and it all made her feel sexier. Harold thought to himself that he had never had the opportunity to talk while getting laid. Mary always just wanted him to get on top and get it over with. He was falling for Charleen with each moan. He knew this was wrong, but he didn't know how to stop, it felt so good. He thought it should not be a sin or a crime to feel this good. Harold took each of Charleen's breasts in his hands and he fondled her. He pulled out the oil that he had put into the warmer in preparation for this moment and slathered her with it. Charleen squealed and laughed and whimpered. He moved his hands so that he could replace them with his lips, and he teased until her breaths increased and she was arching into him. She leaned over and brushed her breasts against him. Then she leaned over him and took him in her mouth and used her tongue to massage him. He was barely holding on to his control.

Harold moaned, "And to think there was a time I couldn't even get him to stand up, now I can't get him to stay down when thinking of you."

Charleen sighed and kept her focus on Harold and how she could make him feel, and how much power it gave her.

"Okay, Charleen, you win."

Charleen looked up at him in the sultriest way he had ever seen. He sat up on the massage table and had her stand. At first, she didn't know what he wanted, but she adjusted the height of the massage table to where she could just slide down on him while he was sitting on the edge. He felt so good inside her. Harold had her slide up and down, and she got more excited with every glide. She knew she was on the edge of shattering, but she wanted him on top. It felt better. She negotiated a change of position. They were barely in a new place when Harold lost control and he made a thrust into Charleen that ignited her. That was all Charleen needed and she let her mind go and with it began one orgasm and then another that was better than the last. They moaned together in delight as the spasms overtook them. Charleen felt the pleasure higher than she had ever thought possible and she did not want it to end.

That is what people must mean when they say they peaked, she thought.

Harold caressed her face and ran his hands up and down her side. Each was in their own world of passion, and each wondered how to capture this moment because it was the happiest either had been in an awfully long time.

Meet the Deceased

Sarah and Kathy were sorting the files from the hospital and those from Dr Canon and pairing them. There were only three men. The first man, Mr Jordan, and then Mr King and lastly Mr Verne who had died a month ago. The rest were women of various ages over seventy years old.

Granger Jordan, aged eighty, had moved to South Florida three years ago. He was admitted to Mercy with flu symptoms and it was noted that he had high potassium upon admission, and he was dehydrated. He lingered for a week in the hospital with supportive therapy but died at the end of eight days. Granger lived in an assisted living facility but was active. He played tennis; he participated in yoga and other activities outside the assisted living facility. His grandson was the only family member and he lived in Tampa. The grandson was with him when he died. There was a living will and a medical power of attorney that named his grandson as his health surrogate.

Hannah Overman, aged seventy, had moved to South Florida a year ago and was presumed to be in good health before being admitted to the hospital with the flu symptoms, and leg pain. She died within five days. She did not smoke; she walked daily according to the records. She worked out at a gym and was noted by her caregiver to like to go the spa and to have massages. Her niece was the only living relative and she lived three states away. It appeared the niece was notified when Hannah was admitted to the hospital, but she did not come to the hospital.

Martha Bright, aged seventy-five, had moved to South Florida approximately a year ago after the death of her husband. Martha was hospitalized four days before she died. She did not smoke; she lived with her dog and three cats. She was a vegetarian. She was reported to have been into wellness and yoga. She had one daughter. The daughter lived in South Florida but was out of town at the time of her mother's death as "it was unexpected" to quote the daughter.

Carmine Windsor, aged seventy-three, was a widow. She had moved to South Florida about two years ago. She was in the hospital for two days before dying. Her symptoms seemed to be more advanced when she was admitted to the hospital than some of the others. There wasn't a social history other than that she lived alone and had a nephew in Ohio.

Those four individuals represented the profile of most of the twenty-six that were on the list of suspicious deaths. There were only three men among the twenty-six. Mr Jordan and Mr Verne had flu symptoms and were tested for both influenza and heavy metals. Mr Verne's results were positive for the flu. Mr King, who was number twelve, died of arsenic poisoning and two others were identified with high arsenic levels. Though it was possible the first eleven might have had arsenic poisoning.

"It seems unlikely," Kathy pointed to the files, "that Mr King belongs with this group."

Sarah responded, "I know. Remember that song: which of these things is not like the other?"

"No, I don't remember ever singing that."

"Well, you have to figure out which thing is not like the other, one of these things doesn't belong, before Ernie finishes the song," sang Sarah.

"I was pretty sure that was the point," retorted Kathy, "but you must have a point about the murders, or we wouldn't be singing Bert and Ernie songs at midnight. Right?"

"Right, you just said Mr King had a wife and a family. Not one of these other people had a living spouse, at least based on the information we have, and Mr Jordan is the only male who did not test positive for influenza. Mr Verne did have the flu. Maybe none of the men were murdered but all the women were? Well, that's not right, Mr King was probably murdered because of the arsenic. We don't know for sure about Mr Jordan, but he might have just died of natural causes, even if eighty is the new sixty."

"You might be on to something. Let's focus on the social history of all the women. It seems that they all had only one relative. Most all of them had moved here within the last few years, if not within the last year. Many of them are reported to have been healthy and even thriving. What are we missing?"

Chloe looked up from her fake bone and walked to Sarah and nudged her hand. "I think Chloe needs to take a break outside," she said. "It's late; should we work more on this tomorrow after class? We also need to go to search Ruth Morgan's place and see what we can find."

"Correction, I need to go to Ruth Morgan's place and see what I can find. You can come up here after class. I will tell the front desk assistant to let you in when you arrive. Let's wrap up for the night. We are at a good place to stop."

"Oh, oh, oh, I almost forgot to tell you!" exclaimed Sarah.

"Oh, oh, oh, almost forgot to tell me what?"

"Are you making fun of me?" Sarah asked, sticking out her lower lip.

"Oh, oh, oh, not at all." Kathy grinned.

"I got the weirdest text today. There can't be anyone outside of Doctor Canon or the director who know I am working on this with you, is there?"

"No one else, but my boss, knows that I am even working on it. Let me see the text."

Sarah pulled out her phone and Chloe started to whine that puppy whine that was an indication she really needed to go out.

"Here's my phone. I pulled up the text for you. I am going to take Chloe. Meet us outside."

Kathy reviewed the text about meeting someone at the gym tomorrow. She closed the office and hurried outside to Sarah.

"Sarah, I have no idea what this is. Are you sure it isn't about something else?"

"I have no idea what it means or who it is from. I do not recognize that number. Can someone in your office find out who it is tomorrow? Do you think I should go to meet the person?"

"I will have the number tracked and find out who it is that owns the phone. I will go with you to the gym. How are you supposed to know who to meet?"

"My guess is the person knows who I am or knows what I look like? Maybe they are going to call me at the gym and see what phone rings."

"I saw that in a movie once," blurted out Sarah and Kathy at the same time. Only Sarah was laughing, and Kathy was groaning.

"I'll also have the tech who tracks the phone find a photo for us," said Kathy. "I'll talk to you tomorrow."

"Good night, Kathy. Come on Chloe, let's go home."

A Visit to the Senior Living Community

Kathy followed up with the tech in the morning and gave her the phone number from the text message that Sarah received.

"Please track this phone number, and then find out all you can about the person who owns it. Also be sure to include a photo. I need it by the end of day. I'll stop back later to see what kind of progress you make. Thanks."

Then she headed off to get a warrant to search the domicile of Ruth Morgan. Kathy hoped to find a clue to move the investigation forward.

It did not take long for Kathy to secure a warrant and head to the senior housing community where Ruth Morgan had lived. Once she arrived, she found the director and provided the warrant and asked to be let into Ruth's apartment. Once inside she looked around to see what might seem out of place. Nothing — nothing was out of place. It was a neat one-bedroom apartment. There was nothing to suggest foul play at least on the surface. Kathy saw a desk in the corner and went to it to search for doctor appointments, a family to contact, a last will and testament, or any sign that Ruth might have been ill. Kathy found a will tucked into a file drawer. It was dated within the last six months. The will named the Mercy Hospital Foundation as the recipient of the proceeds of her estate once the apartment complex had received the money to fulfill her obligations.

Hmm, that was interesting. If someone at the hospital knew that a person was leaving the foundation money, that gave them a motive. She wondered how much Ruth had.

Kathy did not see a computer but there was a tablet. It might have her banking information on it. She would take that back to headquarters. She searched for more evidence that might support that Ruth was indeed murdered. She found her bank account information. There was approximately two million in the account.

"Wow, that makes this even more interesting that Mercy Hospital Foundation is the recipient. That amount of money could go a long way."

Kathy continued to search, and she found an appointment book. She put that in an evidence bag along with the tablet for Sarah and her to review later. Kathy saw a bottle of potassium, a bottle of amlodipine (5 mg) and a bottle of vitamins. She collected the prescription bottles and put them in a bag. She would have to ask Sarah what these things did and why Ruth would be taking them.

Kathy looked around for more clues in the desk, and other places in the apartment, including the bathroom and kitchen drawer to see if Ruth kept anything hidden there. Finding nothing else of interest, Kathy asked the director to close and lock the room.

"Don't let anyone in but me or Doctor Canon from the medical examiner's office. I'll let you know when it isn't considered a crime scene any longer. Thank you for your time."

"Thank you, detective. I will make sure that I keep the extra keys locked up in my office. We all liked Ruth. We will miss her. Did you find anything that you believe might be useful?"

"I did find some pieces of evidence that may be helpful, but I am afraid I cannot share that with you. Try to keep the gossip among staff to a minimum. Before I leave, you can answer this question. Who would want to kill Ruth? Have any other residents died recently?"

"Detective, we are an assisted living facility. Someone dies at least once a week."

"But reasonably healthy people? I have been told that Ruth was healthy and maintained a social life."

"Yes, detective, reasonably healthy people who are old, still have health issues and none of us gets a pass on death. If you mean is there anyone else who died with the same symptoms as Ruth, let me think. As to whether there is someone who would want to kill Ruth, I can assure you that she was well loved among the staff and I can think of no reason why anyone would want to murder that sweet old woman."

"Director, it will be helpful if you can think of anyone else who died with the same symptoms, especially if they were taken to Mercy Hospital."

"We are very close to Mercy Hospital; anyone who needs hospitalization or to be transported by ambulance goes to Mercy."

"Here is my card. If you think of anything that will be helpful, please call me."

"Thank you, detective. Good luck."

Kathy headed back to the office with the evidence from Ruth Morgan's place. She dropped it in her office with the rest of the case evidence and files. She headed over to the tech to see what information she had found on the phone number. "What did you find?"

"I found this information. Her name is Gina Portense. She is a VP at BOTS Inc., a company that makes robots. She lives in downtown Miami in a condo overlooking the bay. She has two cats: one named Spooky and one named Spanky. She is six feet tall, weighs a hundred and ninety pounds, her heart rate is seventy-eight beats per minute on average and in some photos, she is blonde, and in some photos, she is a brunette. Which one do you want?"

"Spooky and Spanky?" Kathy laughed and thought to herself it was too bad Sarah wasn't there. She would appreciate those names.

"Yes, ma'am," said the tech, remaining serious.

"Thank you. That is more information on some levels, and less on others than I was hoping for when I asked you this morning. Do you have an address for her?"

"Yes, ma'am. Here is a sheet with all the information for you, including the IP address of her home computer and the one in her office."

"Thank you. How did you get the IP?" Kathy paused. "Forget I asked; I don't want to know. Thank you and good job. I'll take both the blonde and brunette photos."

Kathy's phone chirped.

Sarah: OTW to the gym.

Kathy looked at her watch and realized that this time she might be the one who was late if she did not wrap up and head to the gym. She locked her office and headed to Star Fitness.

An Uncomfortable Encounter

Sarah got to the university in the morning, but wished she was with Kathy going to look through Ruth Morgan's home. She was in her office when Charleen came to the door to speak to her.

"Charleen, can I help you?"

"Hi, Professor Sandling. Do you have a minute for me to speak to you?"

"Sure, Charleen, come on in and have a seat. It's almost time for me to go to class so it will need to be quick."

"Professor Sandling, I have been doing some research on plants that are poisonous since you gave us that assignment. I find it fascinating, but I am interested in research at the basic chemistry level of plants. I am wondering why we have spent so much time on the topic of poisonous plants. We seem to be missing some information that is required in the other parts of the syllabus. I am worried that we will be held responsible for the material even though we have not covered it in class."

"You are correct, Charleen, you will be responsible for that material. You are in graduate school. It is important in the field of study that you are pursuing that you understand and have skills in various aspects of the biology and chemistry and toxicology of medicinal plants. You may also have the opportunity for researching and developing new drugs. There is more to that research than what plant does a drug come from and how does it need to be processed for human consumption. In addition, now is a time when many people have turned to natural products for achieving or maintaining wellness. There is quite a lot that is right about the natural products industry. But there is very much wrong with it. So, yes you are responsible."

"I don't see why you are teaching this class then. You don't seem to have the students' best interest in mind; you ask us things that don't have anything to do with this class," said Charleen, as her face began turning the dark red color of beets. "I am going to make sure that you don't teach any more classes in this degree. You are not focused on our class needs. I have been to your office several times, and you are never here. I pay your salary and you need to be available to me."

Sarah was so taken aback she hardly knew how or what to reply to Charleen's ranting.

"Charleen, I am not sure where this is coming from. I do not think this is the time to discuss it. I have a class to get to, and then we have class together following that. I think perhaps you should sit out of today's class until you and I can further discuss your feelings."

"All of you people are alike. You only think about yourselves, and you never think of the consequences to others. I have made sure that other people have paid for how they treated me. You will too," threatened Charleen.

"Charleen, if you will excuse me now, I need to go to class."

Sarah calmly got up and waited for Charleen to move and to exit her office. Charleen was fuming but she did not want to be in this office any longer, so she got up and moved outside the door. Sarah came out of the office and locked the door and moved past Charleen. Sarah turned around to address Charleen before going to her class.

"Charleen, I am not sure what has prompted this emotion in you regarding the course. Everything that we cover is pertinent to the needs of the degree. There are multiple ways to do that. In the end, you are responsible for your learning. I can only facilitate it."

"I will be in class, and you will have to deal with it," warned Charleen.

Sarah finished with both classes for the day without incident. Even though Charleen threatened to show up to class, she did not. Sarah headed to the chair of the department's office to report the incident that occurred with Charleen. Now that she had time to think about it some more, she couldn't understand what set Charleen off. Sarah knocked on the door and was motioned in.

"Doctor Mason, I wonder if I might have a moment. There was an incident with a doctoral student today. She may have already been to your office?"

"No, Doctor Sandling, no student has been to the office. But please be seated and tell me what happened."

Sarah took a seat and recounted the incident to Ken, her boss. He listened intently and when she was done, he asked her what she expected him to do.

"I expect that you will support me. I am doing what is professional and teaching appropriate content. I will admit that I have focused on toxicology in the last couple of classes, which usually only gets about fifteen minutes of time. That is because I have been helping a friend with an interesting case and it seemed a good time for the students to get something real."

"I'm afraid there isn't much I can do. If the student comes to see me, I must listen to her."

"I just want you to remember there are two sides to the story. She threatened a faculty member. Doesn't that bother you?"

"Sure, it bothers me. But there isn't anything I am going do about it; it is a free country."

Sarah got up, nodded her head at Dr Mason, and excused herself. She was livid. She didn't understand how he could take a threat so lightly. She thought to herself, doesn't he read the papers, and listen to the news? In Miami, people use guns to settle less. Sarah pulled out her phone.

Sarah: Kathy what are you doing? Meet you at the gym by six PM Don't be late, lmao.

Sarah went by her house and was taking Chloe out for a quick walk around the block. She was thinking about everything that had happened recently and she realized she hadn't had time to even think about Dirk or how to find him. Maybe that was a good thing. During the walk, her mind also wandered to the strange text. She wondered what it was about. Maybe it was one of the students in her class and they wanted to tell her something about Charleen. If so, they were a little late to the party. Charleen had lost her party hat. She wondered why. It could not be her, could it? She was just the recipient, at a bad time, during a bad day, she hoped. "Chloe, you may need to protect me. Can you do that?"

Chloe looked up at Sarah and tipped her head to the side. This was a universal German shepherd action and look. In response, their owners think it is an indication that the dog has understood.

Sarah kept the same philosophy and looked at Chloe. "It's time to go home. I should try and be on time to the gym, if not early, to meet this mysterious person. I wonder what Kathy found out about them."

Sarah left Chloe to 'guard the house' and headed to the gym.

Gina's Plan Unfolds

Gina and China arrived at the gym and signed in and headed to the locker room. Gina was hoping that Sarah would come. Gina was not sure if she got a strange text like that what she would do. She was hopeful that Sarah was curious and would come to meet her. If she did not, then Gina would have to come up with another plan. China noticed that Gina seemed a bit distracted.

"What is up with you, girl? You are somewhere else."

"China, you will never believe what I did."

"What did you do? I promise, I'll believe you." China laughingly threw a towel at Gina.

"Well, I haven't had a chance to tell Dirk about seeing Sarah here at the gym or to give him her phone number because he has been a tyrant recently. It might be all about the girl, but there are other things going on with the business too. So, I have been afraid to tell him, but I am also afraid not to tell him. So, I came up with a plan."

"Why am I not surprised?"

"I texted Sarah and said to meet me here at the gym today. I just said I had information she wants. I didn't tell her who I am or what I want to tell her."

"Really, you just left it as a mystery. How do you know she will show up? I don't think I would."

"China, that is what has me on edge. I hope she does. But what if she does not? What if she brings the police with her?"

"Well, now, I think you are being a bit dramatic. I doubt she will bring the police. Maybe she is the police. Did that cross that twisted mind of yours?"

"You think she is the police? Oh, what have I done? I guess I didn't think this through," said Gina, worried.

"Ya think?" asked China. "On the other hand, maybe she will bring that hot chick that was with her the other day. Maybe she is a cop and likes to play dress up," China doubled over with laughter.

"This is not funny. I cannot believe you are joking about it. What if I made a mistake?"

"Well, you are about to find out, because there they are." China pointed to the girls.

"Kathy, that information that you picked up about the person who sent the text is good. At least we know it's not a crazy person."

"Sarah, I never said she wasn't a crazy person. I told you what she does for a living, and I showed you photos, so that we can identify her today. Hopefully before she spots us. Then we can decide if we want to talk to her."

"Right. I get it. Let's go into the locker room and see what we find."

Kathy and Sarah moved around the corner into the locker room and ran right into Gina. Gina excused herself and then she looked Sarah in the eyes and recognition set in.

She put her head down and attempted to move past the girls quickly. "Excuse me; I am heading into the showers."

"Oh, no you don't." Kathy stepped around in front of Sarah and took Gina by the arm. "You are going to come with me and my friend and tell us exactly how you got her phone number, why you sent her a text, and what it is you are looking to get from her. Got it?"

"Uh oh, she did bring the police." China quietly leaned into Gina. "You are in for it now, girl."

"Let's go," said Kathy.

All four women headed toward a quieter section of the gym. Gina shook off the hold that Kathy had on her and indicated that she would follow. Kathy led the way with Gina; Sarah and China brought up the rear. Kathy led the group to an area toward the back of the gym where there were tables. She invited them all to be seated with a gesture. Once everyone was seated, Kathy stared at Gina. "Okay, Gina Portense, talk."

"How do you know my name?" asked Gina, confused.

"That is beside the point; you sent my friend a text that you have information. I want to know what it is," demanded Kathy.

Sarah spoke up to try and bring down the tension as Kathy was in full detective mode.

"Hi, I'm Sarah; this is my friend Kathy. You sent me a text and I shared it with Kathy, because I was concerned about who might be behind the text, and what they wanted. She found out who you were for me, from a friend."

"I knew you would bring the cops. I'm China and it wasn't my idea; I didn't know anything about it."

"Some friend you are; could you wait a little longer to throw me under the bus?" said Gina.

"Stop the banter. Back to the matter at hand, ladies," demanded Kathy. "Gina, why did you text Sarah such a cryptic message?"

"If we can all back up just a few steps, I'll explain everything." Gina paused and inhaled deeply. "Hi, I'm Gina. I work with Dirk."

"Shut the front door!" exclaimed Sarah. "My Dirk?"

"Well, I don't know if he is your Dirk. But he told a couple of us at the office that he ran into a woman with a dog but did not get her name. Do you have a dog?"

"Yes," responded Sarah. "I have a German shepherd named Chloe."

"That's exactly what he said. He has been trying to figure out how to get a hold of you. By chance, when China and I were here the last time, I heard you telling the story to your overzealous friend here," sneered Gina. "It seemed like you were the person he was looking for.

He said that he had gotten the name of the dog. He said he was going to go walk up and down the street from the Tri-Rail until he ran into you again. He has not been in a great mood since he ran into you."

"Oh." Sarah's shoulders sagged. "I was hoping to have made a better impression on him."

Gina tenderly touched Sarah's arm. "You misunderstand. You did make a good impression on him. He wants to find you. I got your number from the sign-in sheet after I heard you telling the story about running into a man. I thought at the time that you were the person he has been talking about. I was going to give him your name and number, but he has been in such a bad mood that I have not had the chance. I am afraid he will be mad because I didn't tell him right away."

"Yeah, and she got the bright idea to make it a mystery and text you so you can call him, and she won't get in trouble," explained China.

"China, do you mind? I was getting to that part of the story."

"Well, you were taking too long. We are all going to be five years older if I let you finish."

Gina continued. "As I was saying, I thought I would give him your number and then he would call you. But, now that it has been a little while, I am afraid he will think I had some other reason for not giving him the information."

"Yeah, like you'd rather jump his bones than have someone else do it." China was watching Kathy.

Gina blushed and continued on with her story. "I will admit to you that I do think he is a very handsome man. There is nothing between us because Dirk has strict rules about not dating people he works with at the office and he thinks of me like his sister. My career is more important to me than some man, despite what China thinks." Gina glared at China, and then winked.

Sarah looked stunned and was speechless, so Kathy spoke up.

"What you are telling us is the information you have is about this Dirk that Sarah ran into while she was walking Chloe? You don't have information about the murders?"

"What murders?" asked Gina.

"Oh, this is getting juicy," China observed. "I knew you were a cop!" she exclaimed.

"I am not a cop. I do — other stuff. It is a relief that you are here to tell us about this Dirk. So, go on if you will."

"Dirk is the CEO of the company called BOTS," explained Gina. "I am his VP for marketing. Our offices are on Brickell downtown in the financial district. I have worked for him for several years, and this is the second company I have helped him start. We all went out for a drink one night after work. He droned on and on about this beautiful woman."

"He called me beautiful," interrupted Sarah.

"Yeah, go figure," Gina smirked. China slapped her. "You must be his type. He told us you ran into him and you were chasing your dog. He said he forgot to get your name or even how to get a hold of you. He has been moping since then. When I heard you tell the story to the fanatic here, I thought I could help you get together. I am sorry about the text. That probably wasn't the right way to go about meeting you. I just didn't want you to run away."

Sarah interrupted again. "Run away? Why would you think that?"

Kathy had lightened her mood by this time and chimed in. "Run away? She was willing to make a drawing of him and put it up on posts like he is a lost puppy."

China and Gina broke into laughter.

"That is funny. Did you consider the side of a milk carton option?" asked China.

"I know you all think you are funny. Milk cartons are serious business. I would have only done that if the signs didn't work." Sarah said, laughing.

All four women were laughing at the thought of signs and milk cartons with Dirk's photo on them. Kathy recovered from laughing first and said, "So are you giving Sarah the pertinent details or what? We have to get to our workout because I have to get to the office."

"You have to go to the office this late in the evening?" asked China. "What do you do? Also, can I have your number?"

Gina interrupted. "I will give you the details, Sarah. I will give you his office phone and his cell phone. But you might want to call the office and leave a message for him. He might not answer his cell phone if he doesn't recognize the number."

"Wait, what am I supposed to tell him about how I found him?" asked Sarah.

"You can tell him that I gave it to you. You just do not have to tell him how long it was from when I first heard you talking to when I gave you the number. You also might want to skip the secret text part if you don't mind."

Sarah laughed. "I can do that. I do not know how long it has been, so don't tell me. Here let me put his information in my phone. What is it?"

Gina gave Sarah the information.

China worked her way closer to Kathy, while Sarah and Gina were exchanging information.

"So, I was serious about getting your number. You seem like someone I might like to get to know."

Kathy gave China a look up and down and back up that gave her tingles all over.

"I think you must be a very nice woman, but I am not sure what you are asking me…" said Kathy.

"I'm asking for your number so I can call you and ask you on a date. Unless I have misread you?"

"I work out here at the gym in the mornings mostly. I will see you around here. Let's leave it at that for now. I am busy, and not ready to have a relationship. I'll be happy to work out with you here for now."

China considered and asked Kathy, "What time do you work out?"

Once all the information had been shared, Gina announced it was time for her and China to leave.

Sarah figured that since they were at the gym, she and Kathy might as well work out for a bit. The women bade each other goodbye and Gina and China headed out of the gym. Sarah and Kathy headed to the locker room to pick up the weights. Sarah was grinning. Kathy was deep in thought.

Fires in Plano

Tim reached the fire chief in Plano on the phone. The chief told him that the fire did not destroy the home of Betty Carmichael. He also told Tim that there was a niece that he could contact for further information. The chief reviewed the records with Tim and told him that there was no evidence of any kind of a robot or EYE BOT in the records from the fire. The records indicated that the fire was started by a faulty electrical outlet that had an old extension cord plugged into it. There was more smoke damage to the house than fire damage. The woman who lived there was taken out of the house by a neighbor who saw the smoke and called the fire department. It was a small town, and so the chief offered a bit of information to Tim about the house.

"The house was repaired, and the owner moved back into it about a month later. It was now for sale as the owner passed and left all her estate to the Foundation for the Blind. It seems it was a windfall for them, or so I heard on the grapevine. Not to be confused with Grapevine, Texas."

"Excuse me?" Tim inquired.

"That's a little joke that we make here in Texas about the town down the road a piece."

"Oh," responded Tim. "Is there anything else that you think I need to know, chief?"

"I'll send you the report if you give me your email. Then you and your boss can see if there is."

Tim provided the information and thanked him for his time. Tim thought to himself, this was just so strange. He knew the EYE BOT was there. In fact, he believed it was on the list of BOTS that had some sort of difficulty early in testing. But maybe he was just remembering the fire. He pondered what to do next. Tim walked over to see Greta. "Hi, Greta. Do you have a minute?"

"Hi, Tim, sure I do. What can I help you with today?"

"Do you have that letter from the Baronsky and Hart offices? I need to see it for Dave to review. Also, do you know if Doctor Keene got a hold of them, and if anything came out of the conversation?"

"I will get you a copy of the letter. I do not know if he had a conversation with anyone there. He told me that Dave is taking care of it."

Tim moved toward the door. "Thank you. That probably means he didn't speak to anyone."

Greta pointed down the hallway. "You may want to go see Pat, the attorney. Maybe she should be the one to call the offices and find out what is going on. She can speak the lawyer speak. Also, they may have a copy of the letter that she sent to the family telling them that the company would pay for temporary housing."

Tim stopped in his tracks and turned to Greta. "She did what? Why did she do that if the BOT didn't cause a problem?"

"Well, that is why Dirk is mad at her, but you did not hear that from me! Apparently, Dave offered verbally, so Pat just put it in writing, which is very different than a verbal offer that gets turned down."

"Thank you, Greta, for this copy of the letter. I will go to Pat's office now."

Tim left and went to Pat's office to see what she had to say. He knocked on the door to Pat's office and peeked in. She was not there. He was unsure if he should walk in and leave her a note, so he returned to his office. He called and left a message that he had a question about the case of the Carmichael EYE BOT in Texas. Tim pondered what to do next as Dave came back into the office.

"Hi, Tim, how is the search going for the cause of the lawsuit?"

"Not very well if you want to know the truth. I have talked to the chief in Plano and he is sending us a report. I have the letter from the law offices. I stopped by Pat's office and she was not in. I left her a message to see if she would call the lawyers that sent the letter to see if they are serious about suing."

"Good work, Tim. Did you make all the calls to the customers about the BOTS that had the math problem and the updates?"

"I did, but Pat spoke to me after Ms Portense told her I was making those calls and told me that we need to have them sign specific paperwork. She said she will get it to me as soon as possible. Back to the fire at hand, I think that we need to find the niece of Mrs Betty Carmichael in Plano. Do you want me to start looking for her? You spoke to her after the fire, correct? Do you remember her name?"

"No, Tim, I do not. But that sounds like an excellent idea. See what you can find out and thank you."

Dave Takes a Stand

Dirk was in the office early. He asked Greta if she had made that appointment for him for the massage. She replied that she had. "The therapist's name is Harold Pinter," she pronounced it with a long 'I' like 'ice'.

Dirk looked at her and said with a question, "Spell that for me?"

"Pee eye in Tee ee ah."

Dirk thought to himself that he was not sure what the man's last name was based on that spelling. Maybe he could just ask for Harold. Instead, he went for it, because sometimes he just liked to tease Greta about her accent that was unidentifiable, but definitely not from South Florida. "Painter, like a painter, or like a pint of milk, or Pinter like the playwright?"

"There is a Harold Pinter who writes plays? Have I seen one?"

"Yes, he was a celebrated playwright; he is dead. I doubt you have seen anything, but here goes. Have you seen 'The Homecoming'?"

Greta thought for a second. "No, I don't believe I have. Well, anyway it is not him who is giving you the massage. Just ask for Harold."

"As I thought," replied Dirk. "Put it on my calendar and the address. Thank you."

Dirk headed to Dave's office to see what was going on with the fire and the lawyers.

Tim was on the phone, straightening out the customer service issue with the math. He saw Dirk and waved him on into Dave's office.

Dave had been waiting to speak to Dirk but decided it was best to let it happen on Dirk's terms. Sometimes that was the best way to deal with him, since 'the thing'. Dirk walked into the office and smiled.

"Good morning, Dave, how are we this morning?"

"Dirk, I am good. How are you, if you are part of the we you just asked me about?" Dave laughed.

"I'm glad you are good and can laugh at all of this. I was referring to how is the investigation coming along?"

"Oh, you should have said so. I thought since we are friends you would be interested in my personal health."

"Okay, I get it; I have been a bit of a dictator for a little while. What can I do to make it up to you; take you golfing and have a few laughs and a drink or two? I could use that myself. What about if I have Greta call and get us a tee time at the club?"

"I am scheduled to go to Texas this afternoon. I am afraid golf will have to wait. I am taking Tim with me. We are going to try and find the niece of Betty Carmichael, the woman who allegedly died after the fire. Pat got me an appointment to meet with the attorneys in the morning."

"Great work, Dave. I thought she died for sure. You said allegedly?"

Dave exhaled and then inhaled while counting to ten. "You know what I mean. She is dead. She allegedly died in the fire."

"You see, Dave, as I have been saying all of our lives together, the choice of wording is important."

"Here's some wording for you; quit being a jerk. I need to go back to work. I hope you find that woman soon. You are making us all crazy. Maybe you should just go golf without me. The office staff could use a break!"

Dirk turned to leave and wondered if maybe Dave had a point. He thought to himself, I need to find that girl.

Tim walked into Dave's office. "Our tickets are secured for the flight this afternoon to Dallas. I have a rental car and we can go to Plano and stay at the hotel there. I have not had much luck finding out who the niece is. Did you remember her name yet?"

"No, Tim, I wish I did. She was at the house with Mrs Carmichael when I went after the fire. I met Mrs Carmichael very briefly. I am telling you, she did not seem the least bit affected by the fire. She was old but she seemed well, except for being a bit shaken up about being taken out of her house. Being blind and having that kind of urgency happen must make it difficult to adjust. I don't know how the fire could be the cause of her death. She was speaking to me, although she was slightly confused. I chalked that up to the fire. She did not remember using the BOT. The whole thing is strange. Nothing adds up. It is a good thing that we are going out there to meet with the lawyers. I wonder if Dirk is right, if the letter from Pat made the family think that there is something to be gained by suing us over a BOT that they say doesn't now exist because it burned up in a fire. I am having a hard time wrapping my head around the timetable of events."

Tim replied, "That makes two of us. I have been trying to find the niece, but any contact numbers that the fire chief had are not working numbers now. Everything in the records refers to one woman as the niece. There was also another woman that must have been the caretaker. Her name is Flora Jones, or maybe she is the neighbor. I have not been able to reach her at the number that is in the report. I hope that we can find her when we get to Texas. Hopefully, either this Mrs Jones or the attorneys will be able to give us the name of the niece."

"I guess we will see when we get there. Go home and pack your bag if you have not. I'll be by in the car to get you to go to the airport."

"Thank you, Doctor Johnson. I'll see you in a little while," said Tim as he packed up to leave the office. He thought to himself on the way out, who would have thought he would get to be a detective working at a robot company. This was so exciting.

Closer Than You Think

Sarah and Kathy were in the office, going over notes from the hospital. They were still trying to find some link between each of the women.

Kathy told Sarah, "I called Doctor Canon. I told him that Mr King was probably murdered, but that we do not think he or the other men are part of the same case as the women. I also told him that you think that Mr Verne died of natural causes due to the influenza since it was reported he tested positive. What do you think about the third man, Mr Jordan?"

"I also think that he died of natural causes. He was active, and the notes indicate he played tennis. He probably got dehydrated. Once that happens it can look and feel like influenza and he could have had high potassium, especially if he drank some of those sports drinks. Maybe he drank a lot of grapefruit juice or orange juice in addition. That could have added more potassium to his body. One would think that he would have recovered with fluids in the hospital. But maybe he was far enough gone, or maybe he had a little heart attack that no one caught. I know Doctor Canon did not report any heart disease on the autopsy. I think he is being led down a path, and Mr Jordan just happened to be in the mix," said Sarah.

"Okay, then let's focus on the women, unless the next victim that Doctor Canon calls us about is a man."

"I definitely agree." Sarah distracted herself with a file. "I have had a few strange days at school. I have not had a chance to meet with my friend John about the toxicology to see what things we should consider aside from arsenic and some of the plants I have mentioned. Did I tell you about what happened the other day?"

"No, you didn't. What happened?" inquired Kathy intently. She wasn't the anxious type, but she really cared about Sarah. Kathy was used to working alone in recent years. She remembered back to her Navy days. In the Navy everyone had your back, and you had theirs. It was enjoyable to be working with a team member again, mused Kathy.

Sarah waved her hand in front of Kathy's face. "Earth to Kathy — am I boring you?"

"No, go on with what you were saying."

"Well, I was in my office thinking about what the poison might be and doing some research. Charleen, one of the students in my class, who is always a little intense, came by to talk to me. She got very agitated. It did not end well. She said that she was going to get me fired, essentially. I went to talk to my department chair after the class was over and he didn't provide any support. Charleen avoided going to class after the incident. I am not sure what to think. We have class

165

again tomorrow. I have not heard from her. I am a little concerned about what will happen if she comes back to class."

"What did she get agitated about?"

"She said, that I was spending too much time trying to get the students to research and discuss poisonous plants and other poisons. She said she wants to be a researcher and that I am not teaching the class members what they need to know."

"That seems odd. There must be something else. Do you know anything about this woman?"

"No, I don't. I only have access to her name, and school record number because that is how we report grades. I am not allowed to get any other information due to privacy laws. Her name is Charleen Parker. I know she lives somewhere in the area. She has been very guarded in class. I do not even know what she does for sure, but I overheard that she works as a massage therapist. Some of the other students have told me what they do for work. She did say something one time to one of the other students about having moved here from somewhere else, but I did not catch any more of the conversation. Do you want me to ask her?"

"Absolutely not. I do not want you to be alone with her at any point. I want you to run your phone recorder if she says anything to you. I want you to stay as far away from her as possible," stressed Kathy.

"Well, that is going to be a little tough since I am the course professor. I can't give it up; there is no one else who can teach this material in the college."

"Then you are going to have to make sure that you always have someone around. If I need to start coming to school with you, I will."

Sarah opened her mouth, but nothing came out; her eyes flickered intensely as she found the words to respond. "I don't think that is necessary. I do not need a bodyguard. She is not dangerous. She was just blowing off steam that day. I am sure it will be okay when I see her again. Maybe she broke up with her boyfriend. Everyone always has a reason for being ugly to another person."

"You, Sarah, are too nice. In case you have not noticed, there are bad people in the world. In fact, we are trying to find one or more bad persons who are killing innocent old ladies, it seems."

"Don't forget about the man, Mr King. Do you think his wife did it?"

"The wife definitely should be a suspect. But I don't understand why you would poison someone who you have been married to for as many years as the report says they were."

"I don't know. Can you imagine living with someone for fifty years? That must get under your skin at some point and just irritate you. But I think about my parents, and they are managing okay. Gosh, I hope Mom never decides to ask me how to kill Daddy."

"We are getting a little off track here. We have gone from our case, to your angry student, to your mother killing your father. How do you make those leaps?"

"I don't know. I just do; I guess it's my super power."

"That is what I have come to appreciate about you, Sarah."

"My super power?"

"Yes, your ability to leap tall buildings with a single bound."

"Isn't that Superman? I think I am more like Captain Marvel."

"Funny. I meant I appreciate your ability to put together seemingly unrelated things and make sense of it. Like figuring out that it is really the women we should focus on as victims, not the men. They are just distractors."

"We are starting to sound like a season of 'Law and Order'. It seems like all their victims are women who have been killed by violent crimes." Sarah looked at Kathy with a mischievous grin and said, "You'd have figured it out without me. It would just take you longer because you don't watch 'Law and Order'."

Kathy shook her head in way that said Sarah was not adding anything to the conversation. "So, we have twenty-three dead women; how do we figure out how these deaths are related?"

"I still think that it is either a mercy killing at the hospital, or someone is killing them because they are lonely. I wonder if Mr King was killed by his wife because something was wrong with him. Was there anything in Doctor Canon's report about him having cancer, or other health problems?" inquired Sarah.

"One, we don't know that he was killed by his wife. Two, I think that is a big leap to think something was wrong with him and that someone would poison him with arsenic to put him out of his misery."

"That's my super power, remember — coming up with things that don't make sense — until they do."

Kathy sighed, and she and Sarah continued to look through the files, trying to find something in common. While continuing to look through the files, Kathy remembered that they had not talked about the gym experience. She asked Sarah, "Have you contacted what's his name? The hot-bodied man?"

"You mean Dirk. His name is Dexter Irwin Keene and he has a PhD."

"Like I am supposed to be impressed. We have doctorates," said Kathy, emphasizing the last word.

"Right, a lot of them between us. No, I haven't called him."

"Why not? You have moped around and come up with silly ideas for finding him and now you have his number and you don't call him?" Kathy was incredulous.

"Well, I am waiting for the right time."

"When is there going to be a right time?"

"I don't know. We are working on this case, and there is bizarre stuff happening with the class member Charleen, and I don't have the right clothes to call him."

Kathy laughed. "What did you just say?"

"I said—"

Kathy interrupted. "Yeah, I heard you; I just didn't believe that you said you don't have the right clothes. Are you nuts? Wait, do not answer that. You need to call him."

"What am I going to say? Hi, I ran into you with my dog. I have been looking for you."

"That's a start."

"I don't know. Maybe tomorrow," lamented Sarah.

Secrets and Recognition

Charleen was at MassageMe speaking to Corina, the supervisor. Corina called her into the office to give her the news about Ruth Morgan. Corina began by telling Charleen she had some bad news. Charleen's mind instantly went to her past. She tried not to appear nervous and asked, "What is the bad news, Corina?"

"Ay, dios mio, I don't know how to start. I had a call from someone telling me that Ruth Morgan will not be in any more for her massages. She is your client."

Charleen tilted her head. "I am not sure I remember a Ruth Morgan. She must not be a regular. What happened that she is not coming in any more, and that you brought me in here to talk about it?"

"You are the only therapist she saw. She died. Apparently, she was admitted to the hospital after having been in here the evening before."

"What are you asking me? It seems like you are accusing me of something." Charleen got defensive but tried to hide it from Corina.

"I am not accusing you of anything. Why the sudden anger? I was just answering your questions. I brought you in here to tell you that she died and to ask if you know anything about her or her family. But since you say you don't remember her then there is nothing further for us to talk about."

"Wait, I don't remember her. But, did whoever called you tell you how she died?"

"No, they did not," Corina continued. "You know we had another client that died recently. He was a client of Harold's. Do you know anything about that?"

"Only that Harold told me one of his clients died."

"Do you think it's funny that we have had two clients die in this short time? I have never experienced that anywhere else I worked."

"No, I don't think it is anything to laugh about. I am sure it is just that they are old. Old people die."

"I don't know, and I didn't mean laughing; I meant strange. Sometimes my English isn't good."

"Are we done here? I need to get my schedule set for the next week."

"Yes, we are done. Thank you for coming in. I am sorry your client passed away."

"Whatever," Charleen uttered, as she walked out of the room.

Corina continued to wonder about the conversation. Charleen seemed very cold about the death of Ruth Morgan. She knew that Charleen spoke to her clients during their massage because some had complained to her and she had moved them to another therapist. She must know something about Ruth. Well, no one had come asking about it, so she guessed there was nothing she could do. But she did think she was

172

going to have the front desk make a list of the clients that no longer came in for massages.

Corina called one of the front desk girls to come to her office. When Tracy came in to talk, Corina asked her to shut the door. Tracy believed she was in trouble and appeared worried. Corina noticed and motioned for her to take a seat.

"You are a good worker; don't be worried. I called you in to ask for me a favor. But I don't want you to tell anyone you are doing this for me, por favor."

Tracy responded, "Okay. What is it you want me to do?"

"I want you to go through all the records of our clients. I know it will take a while. But in the computer system you should be able to sort by the clients that have not returned. I want to know the names and phone numbers and addresses of the clients that were regulars and now are not coming any more to get massages. Once you have that list, then I will decide what to do with it. Gracias."

"When do you want me to have this to you?"

"I'd like you to begin work on it now. I do not know how long it will take you. You will have to be secret. Es muy importante that you don't let anyone know what you are doing."

"Okay, I get it. I will try to get it done as quickly as I can. But the desk is often busy. I might not get to work on it very often."

"Por favor, just do what you can." Corina nervously showed Tracy to the door.

Charleen was in the staff room. She was pacing and thinking. This was inconvenient. She needed to make sure that Corina did not suspect anything. She wondered if Harold was killing his clients and why. That would be quite a problem for her. She wondered how she could find out.

Another massage therapist entered the staff room and interrupted Charleen's thoughts. "It's a nice day outside today, isn't it? Odd, seeing you here in the day. No class today?"

Charleen responded, "No class today. I picked up an extra shift." Charleen wondered, should she make a phone call now, or wait? Just then the buzzer alerted her to the arrival of her next client.

Well, I will have to wait, she thought. She pulled the lotion from the shelves of the staff room and placed the one from her pocket safely into her purse and thought to herself, time for you to take a break.

Harold arrived at work and was getting the room ready for the first client of the afternoon. The first client today was new and asked for a two-hour massage. Harold thought to himself that it was a good thing it was the first one, because by the end of the day it was much harder to focus. He knew that Charleen had already been at work for most of the day. He also recognized that today all he was going to have time for was to say hello. Mary expected him home early. Harold was trying to decide the best way to approach Charleen since he knew that just the thought of her turned him on. He didn't want to ruin their well-kept secret. Just then, Charleen walked into the staff room and saw Harold. She mumbled something and rushed out.

Now, what is that all about, wondered Harold. The light alerting him to the arrival of his next client illuminated and buzzed, and he was left wondering what just happened.

Dirk signed in for his appointment at the front desk. Harold walked out to meet him, and they discussed what kind of massage Dirk wanted, and if he had any areas of concern. They walked back to the massage rooms and Dirk made himself comfortable. Dirk responded to Harold's questions. "I really need this massage. I have been too hard on the people in the office. Maybe this will get rid of some of the tension. That's the kind of massage I want, a tension-relieving one." Harold left the room. Dirk disrobed and made himself comfortable on the massage table. He relaxed as he began to think about Sarah and her dog Chloe. He saw her lips as he drifted off into the comfort of the dark room as he waited for the massage.

Charleen caught Harold in the hallway by surprise. She whispered in his ear. "Sorry, my love, I was surprised. I did not know you were working today. I guess I forgot. You make me hot, and I just wasn't prepared." She brushed closer to him and took him in her hand. "Maybe later?"

"Maybe later," responded Harold because what else could he say? He was a man whose lover had just raised his hopes, among other things.

Good Afternoon, Mrs King

Kathy was talking with Dr Canon about the murders. No new cases had been reported in the last couple of weeks. They were in his office and discussed what to do about the three men and the women. Dr Canon conceded that at least two of the men's deaths were probably natural causes. Mr King was most likely murder.

"Kathy, will you go talk to each of the families and see what you can find, since you are working on the case anyway. Maybe start with Mrs King; her address is over on Mindello Street. Here is her phone number and address."

"Have you or anyone already spoken to her? Does she know that her husband had a high level of arsenic? Also, Sarah asked me if he had heart disease?"

"He did have heart disease. But it was not advanced. He had a thickening of the cardiac wall indicating inflammation, which could come from arsenic ingestion. He also had some liver abnormalities and changes in the nails on his hands, as I have mentioned before. All of that could be consistent with long term arsenic poisoning." Dr Canon paused thoughtfully. "Those were in the report. On the death certificate, I put that Daniel King died from cardiovascular disease, most likely associated with abnormal levels of arsenic. I presume that the wife read the certificate."

"Humm, I don't think you should assume that the wife read it. I think she would have asked something about it if she read it. I will go see her. Could he have high levels of arsenic from the Miami-Dade water, or some food? You said the fish have high levels of mercury. Does food have arsenic in it?"

"Find out what was in his diet — also if he took any homeopathic medications. There are some still available with arsenic in them. If the wife is very smart, she may have overdosed him with those."

"Is it possible he just died of natural causes?"

"Kathy, we live in Miami-Dade County. Anything is possible."

Kathy said her farewell and left the morgue and planned her next move.

Kathy: Can you meet me at the home of Mrs King. 1401 Mindello St in about 30?
Sarah: I'll see you there.

Sarah was at the university and it was only a quick drive over to the street where Mrs King lived. She had a few minutes before she needed to meet Kathy. She was in her office putting together some class notes. She was also spending some time on the internet looking for Charleen Parker. Sadly, she was not coming up with much information because she did not even have her birthdate and apparently Charleen Parker was a more popular name than she expected. Since she wasn't getting anywhere with that, she pulled up the phone number for Dirk. She thought about it and decided she did not have enough time to talk to him if he was in his office. She sent a text.

Sarah: Hi, this is Sarah, Chloe's mom. I ran into you on the street a while ago. I don't know if you remember me. I know this is weird, do you want to get together for a drink?

Sarah thought to herself, this is so weird. He probably wouldn't even answer her. What if he did not feel the way that Gina said he did? What if she made that up to make her feel like a fool? What if he wanted to meet her?

On that last thought, Sarah realized the time and gathered her things and headed out to meet Kathy. Sarah arrived at the house just as Kathy was pulling up out front. She walked over to meet Kathy and asked, "So, why are we at this house? I thought we had ruled out Mr King being part of the investigation."

"Doctor Canon asked me to come talk to her. I am wondering if she killed him on purpose or if it was an accident. Let's talk to her."

The women walked to the door and rang the doorbell. They were greeted with a woof from inside the house. A woman appearing to be about eighty answered the door slowly. She opened it only a little bit and the security chain was still on the door. A big wet dog nose was sniffing through the crack.

Kathy showed her badge. "Hello, Mrs King. I am here to talk to you about your husband, Daniel King."

Mrs King quieted the dog. "I don't know who you are. Mr King is not in now. You can't come in until he comes home."

Kathy and Sarah looked at each other, wondering exactly what Mrs King was playing at when she implied Mr King was not home.

"Mrs King, may I call you by your first name," Kathy asked.

"I don't know you girls. I think you should go away."

"Mrs King, I know that there are stories of bad people overtaking elderly women in their homes here in Miami-Dade. I promise you that we are not here for that. We know that your husband Daniel died recently, and we are here to talk about why," replied Kathy.

"You could have read that in the papers if he did die. But he didn't die. He is just out. He will be back. I know he will. He promised he would not leave me. He left Gus here to keep me company when he goes out."

"Mrs King, it would be so much easier to talk to you inside, but since you are not comfortable with that, is there someone you can call who will come sit with you while we talk, to keep you safe," asked Kathy.

"Let me call my son, and see if he thinks it is okay for you to come in." Mrs King closed the door and left Sarah and Kathy standing on her front patio.

Sarah asked, "Do you always have this much trouble when you go to interview people? I thought you were not going to let me go with you. Why did you text me to come here?"

Kathy let out a sigh. "Because I think you have a way of putting stories together, as I said before. I do not think that Mrs King is a danger to you. Besides, when you told me about your student, I decided to keep you as close to me as possible to protect you."

"I told you I don't need to be protected. Thank you for letting me come with you. Do you think we are going to have this much trouble with all of the rest of the people?"

"I have no idea. I should have considered that with all the break-ins and forced entry and impersonations going on that we might meet with resistance. The rest of the women who died did not have spouses. I am not sure who we will be going to see, and we will not show up unannounced. I showed up here without talking to her. She did not answer her phone. I figured she didn't recognize the number," explained Kathy.

"I wonder if she will let us in, and if she is really calling her son. What if she just lets us stand here and is inside waiting for us to leave?"

"That's a good thought. I'll be a little more forceful." Kathy turned and knocked on the door again.

The door opened and the dog nose appeared again only a little further out this time. Kathy put her hand down for the dog to sniff. Mrs King asked to see the badge again. Kathy showed her. Mrs King unlocked the door and invited the women in. She was holding a gun. Kathy looked at her and put herself between Sarah and the gun.

"Mrs King, we are truly just here to talk to you. Please put the gun down. Someone could get hurt. I am not going to hurt you. I just want to ask you some questions about Mr King."

Sarah peeked out from behind Kathy's back. "Mrs King, I am a pharmacist. I am working with the police to see why your husband Daniel died. We just want to talk to you. Would it be okay? I would be much more comfortable if you didn't have a gun pointed at me. Maybe you could just lay it on the table while we talk. Please, I'll even let you see that I don't have a weapon on me."

Mrs King put the gun down and broke out into tears and sobs. The dog Gus was quickly beside her and tried his best to comfort her.

"I am so sorry. I did not mean to scare you. I am alone and you can't be too careful. You must know that as women. I miss Daniel. He said he wouldn't leave me, but he has. Do you know where he is? It sounds as if you might?"

Kathy picked up the gun and checked it for bullets. There were none in the chambers. She moved to help Mrs King have a seat on the sofa.

"Mrs King, we are here because the county coroner asked us to come speak to you. Mr King is dead. He was in the hospital and died. I am deeply sorry for your loss. I am here to talk to you about why he died."

"Oh, yes, I remember. He went to the hospital because he was not feeling well. You will have to forgive me. I miss him. He said he wouldn't leave me."

Sarah spoke up. "Mrs King, may I sit next to you?" Mrs King motioned for Sarah to sit. "What is your first name?"

"It's Ethel."

"Well, may I call you Ethel?" Ethel indicated with a nod that it was okay. "Well, Ethel, I am Sarah. This is Kathy as we mentioned. We are so sorry that Daniel has passed on in his journey. I am sure you miss him. Was he ill for an awfully long time?"

"He wasn't ill. Well, I take that back; when he went to the hospital it seemed like he had the flu. We had our flu shots. You are not supposed to die from the shot. But he must have. I'm not thinking very well."

"Ethel, can you tell me anything about you and Daniel's diet? Do you still cook?" asked Sarah.

"I am not much of a cook. We get a lot of our food and juices from the local senior center. They bring us our groceries. I try to make sure we get our fruits and vegetables from juices. It is important. I cook mostly box dinners like leaner cuisines for us," Ethel, lost in thought, drifted away from the conversation.

Kathy motioned to Sarah to let her ask a few questions. "Ethel, do you have the death certificate for Daniel? Did you read it?"

"I don't know what you are talking about," whimpered Ethel.

Gus was lying on the floor beside her, also whimpering. It was a sad moment as it seemed that Mrs Ethel King had no idea why her husband died. She was either in denial that he was dead, or she played confused very well. She seemed to need medical attention herself.

"Mrs King, can you tell me what a typical day of eating looks like for you?" inquired Kathy.

"I drink a big glass of apple juice in the morning, and then I usually have an egg for lunch with some bread. Sometimes I have some cereal. I have a leaner cuisines meal or other food that I can microwave. Then in the evening I have a glass of grape juice. We like our juice in this house. We didn't have it for a while. But when they started bringing us food we asked if we could have juices. Daniel was a much bigger juice drinker than me. He has a glass of juice with every meal."

"Let me clarify, Ethel. When Daniel was alive, he had a glass of juice, either apple or grape, at every meal, and you drink two glasses a day? Do you know what kind of juice you drink?"

Mrs King responded, "Oh yes, you said he isn't coming back. Are you sure? He said he wouldn't leave me. The juice is in the refrigerator."

Kathy went to the refrigerator and took a photo of the brands of juices, and their ingredients. She motioned to Sarah to join her. "What do you think?" asked Kathy.

"I don't know what to think. But I can tell you my intuition says that she did not kill her husband. I think we need to take the juice, and have it analyzed. It sounds like she drinks it too. She is very confused. I wonder if there is someone to call," Sarah whispered.

Kathy went to Mrs King and patted her hand. "Mrs King, Ethel, may we take one of the open bottles of juice with us? Also, you said you have a son. Did you call him? I wonder if you might need to go to the hospital. You seem confused," Kathy said, trying to comfort Mrs King.

Mrs King stood up and pointed at the door and pushed Kathy. "I am not confused. Get out of my house. Who invited you in here? I am going to call my son."

Sarah intervened. "Ethel, I think that is an exceptionally good idea. May I help you? Where is your son's number; is it in your phone?"

Mrs King calmed down. She handed Sarah the phone and indicated that her son's name was Jeff. Sarah took the phone and copied the number in order to make a call later.

Sarah looked at Ethel and smiled. "Thank you, Ethel. We are just going to take some juice with us. We will come back to see you. It was nice to visit with you. Make sure you lock the door when we go."

Sarah and Kathy headed out of the door with two bottles of open juice in hand; one was apple, one was grape.

Sarah looked at Kathy and said, "Well, that was odd. She is very confused. She needs medical attention. What do you think is in that juice? Or maybe she is in the early stages of Alzheimer's disease, or maybe she has had a stroke. We need to get a hold of that son and get her some medical attention."

"I agree with you; let's go back to the office and get these to the lab to be analyzed. I wonder if we will find arsenic?"

Sarah looked at her phone and realized she had a text. It was from Dirk. She put her hand out to stop Kathy from getting in the car.

"I sent a text to Dirk earlier. He just responded."

"What does he say?"

"I don't know. I am afraid to look."

Kathy grabbed the phone. "I'll look and tell you what it says. 'I have been trying to figure out how to find you, if you are the girl with the dog Chloe. I do not know how you found me. I am glad you did. Can I call you'?"

Sarah was just staring at Kathy with her mouth open.

Kathy grinned and said, "So, you better be telling him to call you."

Sarah paused. "First let me call Jeff King and talk to him about his mother."

"Okay." Then Kathy started typing.

Sarah: yes, I will look forward to talking to you

"Hey, give me back my phone!" said Sarah.

"Meet you back at the office. I think we can pretty much rule out that Mrs King killed her husband. He might not have died of natural causes, but I don't think it was his wife. Maybe the son is poisoning them both. That house is in a high-priced area. Maybe he needs the money."

"Do you always have to think that someone is the bad guy? Maybe no one killed anyone? Did you ever think of that?"

"No, Nancy Drew, that is not how it works. Someone is always planning or committing a murder in my business."

"Hooray." Dirk was practically dancing a jig in his office when Gina knocked on the door to see him.

"What has you so excited that you are dancing around the office like a toddler on sugar?"

Dirk rushed over and hugged her. Gina was not sure how to respond, so she just stood there until Dirk came to his senses and let her go.

"I found her!" exclaimed Dirk. "I found the girl. Or rather, she found me. She sent me a text and asked if I remembered her. Of course, I remember her. I am so happy to hear from her."

Gina replied, "I am sure you are. How did she find you?"

Dirk looked baffled. "I don't really know. I have not talked to her. I will have to find out. To tell the truth, I don't really care. I am simply happy to hear from her."

"Wow, all the stuff that is going on in the office, and you are this excited about a girl. Not that I am complaining, but have you forgotten we are being sued or something like that?"

"No, I have not forgotten. I just don't care right this minute."

Gina was now the one who looked perplexed as she exclaimed, "I had no idea what finding the girl would do to you!" and walked out of the office, leaving Dirk to his happy dance.

Dirk was waiting to hear from Sarah. He turned to look for his phone and saw he had a second new message.

Sarah: I am available to talk now, if you want to call me, I'd be okay with that.

Dirk dialed the number and Sarah picked up.

"Hi, this is Dirk. Thank you for texting me. How did you find me?" asked Dirk about as awkwardly as anyone can start a phone conversation.

"Hi, Dirk, someone gave me your number; they heard me telling the story about how I ran into you. It is nice to talk to you, I think. The last time we talked, you scolded me for letting Chloe run free, when she wasn't really." She blushed, wondering, why did I say that?

"I know a really good place close to where I ran into you. Do you want to meet there tonight for happy hour?"

"I am sorry, Dirk, I can't tonight. But I am free tomorrow night. Is that okay?"

"I will make sure I finish up in the office early. May I pick you up?"

"No, I think it is best if I meet you there. Where should I meet you and what time?" asked Sarah.

"I'll text you the address. How about six p.m.?"

"That will work well; I'll see you then. I look forward to seeing you."

Dirk hung up and sat down at his desk. He realized that he had been more distracted than he should have been, thinking about the girl, Sarah. "Now what do I do, now that I have a name? I'd better check on Dave's progress in Texas."

Awkward!

Tim and Dave arrived in Dallas, got their car and headed to Plano, hoping to find some answers. The report from the fire chief did not provide them with any other information than what they already had. They were headed to their meeting with the attorney at Baronsky and Hart partners at the law office located in Plano. Tim spoke to Pat on the phone while they were driving to the appointment. She indicated that she had not been able to speak to a partner, but she had at least been able to confirm that a partner would be present during the appointment. Pat asked to be conferenced in during the meeting. Tim assured her that they would. When Tim hung up from Pat, the phone rang.

"Dave, it's Dirk. Should I answer?"

"Sure, let's see what the boss is up to today."

Tim answered the phone and Dirk indicated that he was just checking in to find out what they had learned. Tim gave Dirk the afternoon schedule and relayed the message that Dave would call after the meeting with the attorneys and indicated they had not discovered anything new. Before he hung up, Dirk told Tim to give Dave a message.

"What is the message, sir?"

"Tell him I found the girl." Dirk hung up.

Tim looked at Dave, perplexed. "He said, to tell you he found the girl. Do you know what that means?"

Dave laughed. "Yes, yes, I do know what that means. It means he will be in a better mood. Now, let's wrap up this threat from the attorneys and make his day even better."

Tim and Dave arrived at the law offices of Baronsky and Hart. They were escorted to a conference room and provided with the access to the audio system and conferenced Pat into the call. Twenty minutes later, a tall, white-haired, large, domineering man entered with two young associates in tow. Each of the young harried associates handed Tim and Dave cards with their names as well as the card for Mr Larkin Baronsky, the senior partner of the organization. The young attorneys were Matt Kline and Stacy Knott. Matt and Stacy were armed with paperwork and tablets. Once the game of passing cards was over, and everyone had politely shaken hands, they all prepared to take a seat. Matt passed the paperwork around and Mr Baronsky took his seat at the head of the table, directly opposite where Dave had positioned himself. Their choice of seating at the table was a power play on the part of each man. A young woman came in who introduced herself as Linda and indicated she would take notes. Mr Baronsky began the meeting.

"Welcome. Each of you has reviewed the paperwork and understands why we are all here?"

Dave spoke up. "Actually, we don't quite understand why we are here. We tried to get some answers prior to our arrival but were unsuccessful. The letter we received does not indicate anything other than the threat of a lawsuit on behalf of Mrs Betty Carmichael. It is also our understanding that she did NOT die during a fire which was NOT caused by our robot. Let's move past the games."

"My dear fellow, a lawsuit will be filed on behalf of the niece who is representing her aunt who lost her life due to malfeasance on the part of your company. Mrs Carmichael is in fact deceased due to the fire in her home."

Pat cut in on the phone, trying to avoid a blow up from Dave, which she anticipated based on the breathing she heard from him over the phone.

"Mr Baronsky. We investigated the fire when it was first reported to us. We were assured that the robot was not the cause of the fire by the inspector. In fact, we were told that the robot was not even in the home. We were also informed by the fire chief that there was more smoke than fire. We offered to provide support to the family, knowing that Mrs Carmichael was sight impaired and we felt that offering support was the right thing to do. I hardly think you can call our offer to support her malfeasance."

"Your company offered to provide that support because you know that the robot was the cause. I have read the reports that there have been problems with the

EYE BOT. This is just one of the suits that we will bring against you."

Dave blew up. "You're an ambulance chaser with no ethics and you won't get away with this. We came here in good faith to discuss the fact that we are not responsible. There is nothing in the fire inspection report about the BOT having been the cause of the fire. We are leaving. Come along, Tim."

Pat was on the phone trying to get a word in edgewise. "Mr Baronsky, I know that my colleague is preparing to leave. I hope that we can come to an understanding about why this is occurring. It does not seem to involve us, and I can't imagine that you have evidence to the contrary. If so, you need to provide that to us."

Mr Baronsky got up, assessing Dave's imminent departure and indicated to the young attorneys that he was no longer interested in discussing this case. He also turned to leave the room.

The only people left in the room were Linda, who was still trying to take notes, and the two young attorneys who were looking at each other with expressions of 'what just happened' on their faces. Pat was on the phone asking, "Is anyone still there? What is going on?"

Stacy stared at the phone and responded, "Ma'am, they have all left the room. I guess we will see you in court."

Pat replied, "I'd really like to avoid that. Do you have any other paperwork available for me?"

"We do not. Mr Baronsky expected that your company would bring a large settlement offer today and leave us with a check," said Matt.

"Then Mr Baronsky doesn't know who he is dealing with. We will not settle a case for which we are not responsible. We will get to the bottom of this, one way or another. Goodbye." Pat hung up her phone. She then put her head in her hands and wondered, what next?

Tim and Dave were in the car and on their way to dinner. Neither had much to say, because both were pondering what had just occurred. Tim was trying to think of a way to get the name of the niece from the fire chief.

Tim asked, "Should we call Pat? Should we call Dirk?"

Dave, deep in thought, shook his head. "Let's hold off until we have something more than an irrational ambulance chaser. We'll go check in to the hotel and get dinner and discuss our next strategy."

"Do you remember where you met the niece? Has her name come back to you? Maybe I can do a search on her and find something. Her name is not in the fire report, but I will call the fire chief and ask if he knows anything about her. I wonder why the BOT was not in the house?"

"That, Tim is the million-dollar question. The second million-dollar question is why did Mrs Betty Carmichael die, and is there an autopsy? We will need to stay a day or two longer, but maybe we need to hire an investigator. I think we have moved beyond what you and I can do."

Tim put private investigator, Plano into the search engine to see what the options would be. Then he dialed the fire chief again. "Sir, this is Tim again from the BOT company. Thank you for the report. Do you by chance remember the name of Betty Carmichael's niece?"

"Son, I remember that she did not live with her aunt. I remember that she was sort of average looking for a woman. I don't know if I ever knew her full name. To the best of my recollection, it is something like Caly, but it is not Carmichael. She had a different last name. She came here to the station about three weeks after the fire and wanted a copy of the report. Let me see here if I look back, what I can find." There was a short pause while the chief looked, and he put Tim on hold. The chief came back on the phone. "Here it is. We make everyone sign in. Based on the approximate date, I see that her name is Caly Parker."

"Caly Parker?"

"Yes, that's correct. She seemed mighty upset by something the day she was in here. She said her aunt did not know what she was doing, and she would regret it. I wondered at the time what that meant. I read about Betty's passing and turning all that money over to the

Foundation for the Blind. I wondered what the niece thought about that being she was Betty's only living kin. It's a small town; I hear a lot of things I don't really want to. I hope having that name helps."

"Thank you, chief. Do you know if Caly is short for a longer name?"

"No, son, I do not. Best of luck."

"Well," sighed Tim, "Now we have a name at least." He hung up with the fire chief.

Pat got up from her desk in the office and decided she needed to go see Dirk. She asked Greta if he was available and was waved into the office.

"Dirk, do you have a minute? I just got off the phone with the attorney from the firm that is threatening to sue us. They are representing a relative of the deceased Mrs Betty Carmichael. Dave and Tim were present in the office. The call did not go well. It went downhill fast when Dave called the senior partner an ambulance chaser," explained Pat.

"I guess when you say it didn't go well, you mean we don't know what happened to the BOT or to Mrs Carmichael."

"That about sums it up. The senior partner seems bent on taking us to court. I will send a response to the letter indicating that the evidence from the fire inspector's report says that they did not find a BOT present, and that the BOT is not the cause of the fire. I suspect they will still try to take us to court for a large settlement as the young attorney put it today."

"Do what you can to end this quietly. The firm does not need more negative publicity than we have already gotten. When are Dave and Tim returning?"

"I suspect that negative publicity is what they were counting on for us to make a settlement out of court. When Dave and Tim are coming back, that I do not know. I haven't spoken to them since they left the meeting. If you want my opinion, we should not settle. We are not responsible. But as you said, they are holding on to the letter I sent as evidence that we are. I am sorry to have put us in that position."

"You aren't at fault. You and Dave were trying to do the right thing for our customer. It will be okay. Thank you. You can go now," responded Dirk as he stared out the window, distracted by the threat of a lawsuit and by Sarah. For Dirk, tomorrow could not come fast enough.

Permission

Harold and Mary were sitting in the kitchen.

"Harold, I brought home some of the powder you asked for. It is in the closet with the rest of the pottery supplies. You seem distant. Is there anything going on at work that you want to talk about?"

"No, thank you, Mary. I just need to do something to relax. Even though one would think giving massages is relaxing, it can be stressful. I am on my feet all day, and I feel like a bartender. Many people want to get rid of their problems in addition to getting the lumps they get from their problems massaged away."

Frowning, Mary responded, "I guess you get tired of hearing people grumble. I realize we don't talk very much about your workplace. Are there other nice people there for you to be friends with? I know you say you go out with the boys on occasion. I am glad you are making new friends."

Harold wondered how much he should say. "I do have a couple of friends who are also massage therapists. They have similar interests. Thank you for understanding that I need a night or two out with them during a week. You are a very understanding woman."

Harold frowned as he wondered, how understanding would she be if she knew what I was doing with my new friends? He managed to keep his expression neutral as he thought about Charleen. "In fact, I think I may go out after work with them tonight. You will be in bed by the time my shift is over."

"Sure, I think that will be nice."

Harold turned this conversation into permission for his dalliance with Charleen, his beautiful, sexy paramour. Mary got up and kissed Harold on the forehead like his mother did when he was a little boy.

Harold got up and moved to the closet to prepare to throw some clay before he headed to MassageMe for his shift. He needed a distraction, because Charleen was all he could think about. It had been several days since they were last together. He needed a release and then he would head to the office, where he was hoping for another kind of release.

Action in the Back Room

Corina called Tracy into the office when she believed that everyone else was engaged with other work and before the second shift of therapists came to work. "What have you been able to find, Tracy?"

"You aren't going to believe this. I have found about a hundred people who have not come back to the clinic in the last year. About half of those people seemed to be regulars or had been here more than a half a dozen times. About twenty-five of them have moved away and I was able to find them registered at other MassageMe offices around the US. A couple ended their contracts with letters. I am still looking for about another twenty-five of them. It is a little harder to find them. I have not looked for a pattern, if that is what you are wondering." Tracy laid the partial report on Corina's desk. "Twenty-five people doesn't seem like that many when you think about how many people come in here on a weekly basis. Do you want me to keep following up on them?"

Corina thoughtfully responded, "Yes, keep looking to see what happened to those twenty-five. Make sure you also include the therapist they saw regularly in your report. I am particularly interested in that. I have itch at my intuition."

"I don't know what you mean by that, but I will try to finish up this week. I have a test again tomorrow. Do you mind if I go home early again tonight?"

Corina looked at Tracy. "What?"

"Well, one night Harold sent me home early because he said that if I needed to study for a test, it would be all right."

"It is okay with me, but check with Harold. If he has let you do it other nights, I suppose I am okay with it."

Corina frowned. What exactly was Harold doing? She wondered if installing cameras in the rooms was something to consider. It would be a problem if a client found out though, so she let the thought go.

Charleen was headed into the door of the office when she ran into Corina. Corina explained that Tracy would be leaving early. She asked if it would be a problem for Charleen. Charleen could not believe her luck. She had been aching for some time with Harold. It seemed like the fates were with them today. She had packed her car with candles, and some other toys that her girlfriends said they used. She calmly responded to Corina's question.

"Sure, if she has a test, I understand that, being in school myself."

Charleen was on a mission and Tracy leaving early would help further all her goals. She saw a familiar man come in the other day to get a massage with Harold. She had trouble placing him, and she needed to get a look at his name. She was pretty sure it was Dexter Keene from the BOT corporation. She had been wanting to meet him.

Harold arrived in the office to the news that Tracy would be going home early. He had trouble containing his excitement. In fact, he felt that familiar rise of his expectations at the thought, and he needed to find some cover. He excused himself to get ready for his first client. He had been thinking about the rise and fall of Charleen's breasts with each breath she took. He thought about the sweet taste of her essence. He realized that he was now not just rising to the occasion but hard and ready to explode. He needed to find some release now, not in eight hours. He had fifteen minutes until his first client arrived. He saw Charleen walk into the office. She looked like the angel he fantasized about every night. She saw him enter the room and recognized his mutual enthusiasm from the swelling in his scrubs. He placed a finger across his lips to indicate she should remain quiet and moved toward her. He guided her to the storeroom at the back of the offices. This was not exactly how he thought the night would start, but he promised himself to make it up to her later. They moved into the storeroom and he turned to lock the door and bolted it. There was only one other therapist who came in to work for the evening, but he didn't want there to be any chance of discovery. Harold whispered, "I promise to make it up to you later, but I want to be inside you now. I only have fifteen minutes. What about you?"

Charleen found the whole thing more exciting and sexier than she would have ever imagined. She was already wet and ready. "Harold, I'll take you anywhere, and any time." She reached for the drawstring of his scrubs and released his manhood into her waiting hands. "Ohhhhh, Harold. I have been craving to hold you and to put my mouth around you since the last time."

She leaned over and covered him with her mouth. It was almost more than Harold could take. He tried to suppress a groan, but it escaped to the quiet of the storeroom and sounded like the roar of the mighty lion to Charleen. She licked and sucked harder because to her that was the sound of his love for her. He was conquering his feelings and letting them free. Charleen recognized that they only had a short time and she wanted her own release. She quickly moved to take off her scrubs and to let her breasts free. She took Harold and guided him into the chair. She had learned to like this position compared to other ones. They had tried several during their last few encounters. Her world had expanded, and she now accepted and embraced her sexuality as she had never been allowed to. She leaned over him and teased him with her nipples. She held him and settled over him and was lowering herself as Harold took one nipple into his mouth and slurped at it like a he was drinking from a refreshing stream, as he rolled the other into a taut rosy embellishment to her beauty. She was barely surrounding him when she shattered, and Harold felt the pull and tug of her orgasm and followed her into the abyss. They both ascended from their bliss a few moments later and realized that they didn't have time to linger. Harold leaned forward and kissed Charleen — a lingering kiss that promised more to come. They managed to pull themselves together and to make it out of the storeroom unnoticed. Each therapist moved to get to their first clients without raising any suspicion. Both were stimulated by the inherent danger of having sex in the back room. The shift went by quickly, as both were on a high that maintained them through the evening.

They closed the office after their shifts were over.

Charleen set candles around her room. She put oil in the warmer and she changed into something she thought would drive Harold crazy. She pulled out the handcuffs that her girlfriends suggested, and a vibrator. She had been experimenting with it at home. Now she was looking forward to trying it out with Harold. She was pulling thigh high black nylons up as Harold entered the room.

It was dimly lit by the candlelight, but to Harold it was the brightest room he had ever been in because Charleen was there. He felt his heart beating in his throat. He went to Charleen and embraced her from behind. He ran his fingers through her hair and pulled her as close to him as possible. Charleen laid her head on his chest and sighed in a tender moment that she would cherish, for as long as she lived. Harold leaned over, turned her to face him, and gently took her chin in his hand and lifted her face to his. He covered her lips with his and pressed his tongue into her mouth to tease while he raised his hands to her nipples to find them already hard and ready for his touch. Charleen savored the moment. They spent the rest of the evening exploring and savoring their time together. They each made promises they would not be able to keep.

What Could Go Wrong?

Sarah and Dirk were sitting at an outside table. Chloe was with them and laid at Sarah's feet. The two had been sitting for just long enough to order a glass of wine. Dirk played with the stem of the wine glass while watching Sarah blush at his every question.

"I don't know how you found me. I told the people at work that I had run into you, but I didn't have any information for them about you except for the name of your dog."

"I work out at a gym. I was telling the story to my friend. Someone overheard me who knows you. I got a note with your name and phone number. I looked up your name on the internet. You look like the photo I found with your name. Then I went on BusinessConnections and looked at your profile. I found the company name and I looked up more information. I didn't mean to stalk you, I just wanted to know more about you before I sent you a text out of the blue."

Dirk smiled, and it reached his eyes; they twinkled like the reflection of the night sky. "It's okay. I am glad you pursued me. I would have done the same, but I really had no place to start. Tell me about you. What do you do? I am at a disadvantage since you have had a chance to find out about me."

Sarah grinned. "I am a pharmacognocist. I study plants, and research how they might be used for medications. I am also a pharmacist, but I don't practice at the local pharmacy. I work at the University of Miami and teach and do research. I am not like the pharmacists you read about in books though, I mean the crazy ones. Well, that is not what I mean either. I think I'll just stop talking." Her cheeks were rosy, and she was looking at Dirk through her long eyelashes.

Dirks nose wrinkled when he laughed. "I think that is a very noble profession. My uncle owned a pharmacy. I used to help him by doing deliveries when I was in high school. He sold it a long time ago. He said that the business wasn't like the old days. He is retired and living in Barbados. I visit him sometimes. Maybe you could go with me."

"I'd love that." She grinned. "But don't you think you ought to know me a little better, and vice versa? I do like to travel. I speak a couple languages. I went to school outside of the country. What about you? Why did you start the BOT company?"

"It's not particularly exciting. I started the company after I sold my first one. I am an engineer, a biomedical engineer. I went to Rice University for a BS in mechanical engineering and I went to Boston University to get a PhD in biomedical engineering. I want to design robots that will be helpful to people with disabilities.

My first one is called an EYE BOT. We have several in homes, and our first ones do tasks for sight-impaired individuals. They aren't quite seeing-eye dogs, but they can do things a seeing-eye dog can't. Although we had a math problem recently and I think your dog Chloe could have done better at the math than our BOTS. We have since fixed that problem. My mother went blind when I was young, and I realized the problems she had when I was not there for her. That is how I came up with the idea. I have a couple of patents, but I'm just a normal guy."

"Well, we'll see how normal you are. DC or Marvel? Star Trek or Star Wars? Favorite band? Okay, that's a good start."

"Let's see. At least you did not ask me to solve a logarithmic equation, because I don't think I could without a calculator. I am a Marvel guy myself; Doctor Strange is my favorite. Do not laugh. Star Wars because I think Princess Leia is hot in those early movies, even if the wig is ugly. Let's see, my favorite band is Aerosmith. What about you?"

"I am an Iron Man girl. Who doesn't like a rich genius who drives fast, expensive cars? I mean, not that I am that shallow. But he is hard to resist." She giggled, even as she stumbled over what she considered a fumble with that last statement.

Dirk laughed with her. "I get it. I think. Based on that I do not think I will meet your expectations if those are your requirements. I drive a ten-year-old Jeep."

Sarah was flustered, turned bright pink and did not know how to respond. "I wonder where those drinks are?"

Chloe looked up as the waitress came out the door with the drinks.

Sarah got a notification and looked at her phone. It was Kathy texting. "Excuse me." Sarah looked up at Dirk. "I am helping a friend with a problem and she just texted me. Do you mind if I take a moment to see what she wants?"

"No, go ahead. I'll look over the menu, I am hungry."

Kathy: Sarah, I found out information about the juice. Do you have time to come over to the office now?

Sarah: OMG, I'll be there. BTW I am out with Dirk getting a drink. He seems to be a nice man. I wonder what is wrong with him. I'll finish and head your way. Give me 30 minutes? I have to drop Chloe off at home.

Sarah looked up at Dirk. "Did you find something good to eat?"

"I found several things. What are you going to have, a salad?"

"What exactly are you implying? That was pretty rude."

"I just meant all the girls I have dated have a salad when we go out for dinner. Just one time, I would like to go out with someone who isn't trying to pretend they eat like a rabbit. Although some of them might have been rabbits. I'm not sure. Did I get my foot out of my mouth yet?"

"All the girls you have dated. You think they are rabbits?" Sarah stood. "I am not your type. I think that is clear. I'll just be going. No, your foot is solidly implanted on your tongue. I wish I could say it has been a pleasure, but I think we'll go. Have a nice dinner."

Dirk watched Sarah leave and wondered how it all went so wrong. She was a beautiful woman. She was round where she should be, and had lovely full breasts, and just the right amount of bottom. She had blue eyes that seemed to see right through you, her lips were full and luscious, and she stole his heart the day they met on the sidewalk. He shook his head and called the waitress over.

"I'll have two slices of humble pie."

"I'm sorry, sir, that isn't on the menu. We have a pot pie with beef if you want that," said the perky little waitress.

"No, I'll take the spaghetti Bolognese, to go please." Dirk grimaced. At least he had her phone number. He wondered if she would speak to him again.

He got on his phone search engine and looked her up at the University of Miami. He then followed with a call to the local florist to have a large bouquet of long-stemmed roses sent to her office first thing in the morning. He told them to put, 'I'm an asshole. Can we start again, please? I am so sorry. Will you go out with me this weekend? Please forgive me. Dirk' on the note.

Sarah got Chloe into the car and headed for home. She reflected on what just happened. How had that gone so wrong? He did not say she was fat. He just asked if she wanted a salad. She guessed Mom was right. She was too sensitive. If he didn't like her, he would not have gone to all the effort to try and find her. Maybe she shouldn't have been in such a hurry to leave. Oh well, no use crying over spilt milk or something like that. They arrived at home and Sarah took Chloe in the house and put food in her bowl and refilled her water dish. "I'll be back, girl. Guard the house." Sarah scratched Chloe behind the ears as she headed back out the door to meet Kathy at the office.

Juicy Information

Sarah parked the car and headed into the office building. She rang the bell so that Kathy could let her in to access the elevator to the top floor. Sarah was barely off the elevator before she demanded, "What did you find? Also, men are Neanderthals. What did you find?"

"I am guessing, by that comment, that you didn't have any trouble getting away from him. In fact, I might have saved you?"

Stomping her foot, Sarah glared. "I don't want to talk about it. What is in the juices? Is it arsenic?"

"You are correct. A whole lot of it. It doesn't appear that it was added by anyone though. The lab tech went and bought another unopened bottle of the same brand, thinking that what she found must have been in error. Guess what she found?"

"Oh no, she didn't?"

"Oh, yes she did. She found the same amount in the unopened bottles of both grape and apple juice. Did you get a hold of Jeff King yet? You need to, or his mother will be going down the same path as his father quickly. The only thing that seems to have saved her so far, is she drinks less, and she didn't get the flu. I talked to Doctor Canon. He said that probably when Mr King got ill, he was weak, and his levels were probably higher because he drank more. We need to see if any of the names on that list got food and juice from the same food pantry."

"I'm on it. I am calling Jeff right now. I wanted to wait to see what we found out before I alerted him that we were working on his parents' case."

"Good thinking. While you call, I am going to start looking at the list of names and see even at this time of night, if I can get anyone at that food bank. Likely I won't be able to until tomorrow."

Kathy pulled up a google search of grape and apple juice and arsenic concentrations. She found an article that showed that there were brands of apple and grape juice that were reported to have more than the proposed federal limits of arsenic.

Kathy read through the page. There was a federal allowable limit of arsenic? How was that possible? It seems that both children and adults could be at risk depending on the amount that they drank per day. Based on this the Kings were past the limit of safe.

Sarah came back from the side room where she was making the call to Jeff King.

"I got a hold of Jeff. He was shocked and grateful at the same time. He said he will get to his mother tonight and take her to the hospital and tell them relayed to him about the juices and th~ him my number so that if there is any ᴠ physicians, they can call me. At least ᴡ save Ethel. She probably has some heart disease, or liver disease from the chronic use. I asked Jeff to keep us updated about her progress. He said he will."

"Look at what I found about apple and grape juices. We need to contact the food pantry and see what they are serving to both adults and children."

"It hadn't even occurred to me to think about grapes and apples for arsenic. Apple seeds are dangerous if you chew too many; you can get cyanide poisoning." Sarah frowned. "Did you call the food bank?"

"They aren't in until tomorrow."

Sarah moved to sit down. "Let's get to that list. One thing we know is that Ruth Morgan probably did not get her food from there since she lived in that long-term care facility. What we need to figure out is what ties her to the rest of the people."

Sarah was reading the hospital and autopsy reports for social histories as well as going back through the cause of death and descriptions of the bodies. The first man, Mr Jordan, was presumed to have died of influenza even though Dr Canon put him on the list after the appearance of multiple deaths from seemingly the same cause. The autopsy report did not note any abnormalities aside from the usual body changes for an eighty-year-old man. In the medical history it did not indicate that he had had a flu vaccine. Maybe that would have saved him. Sarah continued to make her way through the reports. She was not sure what she was looking for and was trying to see a pattern in the information. She noticed that most of the women over age seventy-five listed contacts in the area but dismissed that as not being anything of importance.

Let's start from another direction, she thought, reframing her thinking. Who did not have an influenza vaccine and might have just died from the flu? She knew that Dr Canon thought about this earlier and concluded it wasn't an influenza breakout. It still seemed like the place to start. She found four women in addition to Mr Jordan that did not have the vaccine; they were all over seventy-five years of age. Hmmm, she wondered. Who else is over seventy-five? She found six more women who met the criteria. She continued to look through the records while Kathy searched the internet for articles on arsenic poisoning.

Finally, Kathy looked up at Sarah, with bloodshot eyes. "I think it is about time we wrap things up. There is more going on here than bottles of juice and the flu. I just don't know what. Let's call it a night."

Sarah nodded. "My head is hurting but I think I am on to something. I really need that list from the food pantry."

Deliveries

The driver pulled up outside the address listed on the Lyft app. The woman in the back seat got out and walked to the door and looked for a place to put the package. There was a dog looking through the window. "Stupid dogs. Why do people think they are so smart? They are just dumb animals," she said.

After a few minutes of looking around, the woman found the right place to put the note and the bottle of champagne and turned to leave. The dog barked one menacing 'woof' and turned and walked away from the window. The car pulled away with the woman inside as she planned her next move. Meanwhile, Chloe continued to guard the house.

Across town, an unmarked delivery van pulled up outside the BOT offices. The driver got out and took a basket into the receptionist.

"I have a package for Doctor Keene. It needs a signature."

The receptionist replied, "I'll sign for it, and I will make sure that it gets to Doctor Keene."

"Thanks. Have a good day," mumbled the driver quickly while he exited the building.

The receptionist made a call to Greta to come pick up the package. "It's a basket of food."

Greta presumed that it was from one of the vendors and took it to the staff lunchroom. The note read, 'carpe diem, quam minimum credula postero.' Greta scratched her head thinking about the note. It was odd; she didn't know who to send a thank you note to for this lovely gift and there wasn't even a delivery company name for her to call.

She took the food out of the basket and placed it on the table. Then she took the cheese and bottle of wine and put them in the refrigerator for later.

A floral delivery vehicle was pulling up outside the University of Miami building that housed the chemistry department. The driver walked in and climbed the stairs, finally finding an assistant in the main office on the third floor.

"I have a delivery for Doctor Sandling."

The assistant, Mike, got up and came over to greet the driver and to take the box. "Should she be worried about a bomb?"

The driver was taken aback with the offensive comment. "Excuse me; I brought the box directly from the florist shop."

"I'm sorry," retorted Mike. "Just some dark humor. Doctor Sandling has a student that is not happy with her, and we have all been hearing about it for several days now. I will make sure that Sarah gets the box when she comes in this morning."

The driver headed back to his delivery vehicle, mystified.

The FedEx truck pulled up outside the condo where Charleen Parker lived. The driver took a package to her door and knocked. He did not get an answer, so he tucked the envelope beneath the mat, took a photo and left.

With Apologies for Bad Behavior

Sarah arrived at the university and was rushing past the main office to avoid any confrontations. It seemed that Charleen had caused a ruckus in the department and today was not the day Sarah wanted to discuss it with her boss. So far, she had only heard the gossip; Charleen had not been back to confront her, nor had she returned to class. Sarah was expecting that any day she would be called into the chair's office for a scolding.

Mike called out to her, "Doctor Sandling, there is a box here from a florist. It's for you."

Sarah stopped in her tracks. She did a U-turn and headed stealthily into the office and looked around for anyone who might try to corner her. The path looked clear and so she stepped in a little further. Mike handed her the box.

She took it, and was about to walk away with it, when Mike grabbed her arm. "Oh no you don't, girlfriend. I want to see what is in that box. Then I want to know why."

Sarah pulled the ribbon from the box and dramatically took off the lid, slowly, making him wait for as long as she could. She really had no idea what might be in the box, but it did look like it was flowers.

Sarah gasped at the beauty of the roses. There were a lot of them.

"Oh, my gosh. Where is the card that came with these?"

"Look inside, because there wasn't a card on the outside, or I would already know who sent them."

"You are so bad," said Sarah, laughing. "Here it is. Oh my, it is from my date the other night. He is asking me out again."

"Let me see that." Mike grabbed the card from Sarah's hand and read, "I was an asshole." He looked over his glasses and down his nose at Sarah and pursed his lips. "Out with it. I want the whole story."

"It's a long one and I have to get to class. I promise you I will fill you in later. In the meantime, are there any more rumors about, you know, that I should know about?"

"You are good; the chair isn't going to do anything. I overheard him tell her if she wants to graduate, she will have to get a passing grade in your class. He didn't exactly support you, but he didn't throw you under the Miami-Dade County bus either."

"See you after class. In the meantime, will you hold on to these? You can even put them in the vase and put them on your desk until I get back. You can pretend they are from that cute stud over in biology that you daydream about." Mike grinned, blushed, and took the roses.

In the Lunchroom

Greta was in the lunchroom with a few other administrative assistants and they were eating the snacks that were in the basket. The cheese was open on the table. They decided to wait to drink the wine until later after work. Greta was talking about the office morale and telling the staff that Dirk had been in a better mood. She was hopeful that his mood improvement would translate into happier executives and happier staff.

Dirk walked in just about that time, frowning. The women all looked at Greta, perplexed because he did not look like the happy man, she described moments earlier. He got a notification on his phone, looked around the room, and stepped back into the hall in case it was Sarah.

Sarah: Thank you 4 the beautiful roses. I am off to class. Will call you when I get out. Sorry I ran away so quickly. Your apology accepted. Yes, to date this weekend.
Dirk: 😊

"Hello, Greta and everyone else. What is on the assistant agenda today," asked Dirk as he stepped back in to the room.

A rather sheepish grin crossed Greta's lips. "How do you know that we have group meetings?"

"Because, Greta, I am the boss, and I am supposed to know these things. Plus, Gina told me," he said, with a big grin that reached to his eyes; he imitated a high five. "I think it is an excellent idea for you to keep the staff informed of all the important business of the office. We want to be a transparent and open office culture." Dirk took a couple of slices of cheese from the table and moved to go back to his office and to check on Dave and Tim.

Greta called him back. "Do you know what the card means?"

Dirk looked and with a hand gesture indicated there was no signature. "Who sent this?"

"I don't know. That is why I want you to look at it. I thought maybe the words would mean something to you. It looks like Greek to me." Dirk examined the card.

"It is Latin, not Greek. It basically means seize the day because you don't know about tomorrow."

"Oh, that seems ominous." Greta looked at the rest of the assistants for support. They nodded in agreement.

"Yes, a little." Dirk grabbed a few more slices of cheese and some crackers and headed out of the door, leaving the assistants wondering what to do. On the way out he exclaimed, "Carpe diem!"

This Cannot Be Right

Charleen opened her door after returning from her errands. She saw the package underneath the mat. She looked at the return address.

Good — this was the beginning of the end. Soon she would have what she earned for all those years of taking care of that ingrate. She hoped the check was big enough for a house in the islands and to support her love and her in a manner to which they wanted to become accustomed. Funny that it hadn't required a signature. She took the envelope into the house and pulled it open. There was one piece of paper. There was no check. She turned bright red. She threw the envelope and ripped up the letter. "They haven't heard the last of me!" she shrieked as the tears ran down her face.

Chloe's Warning

Sarah got in the car and headed home. She called to talk to Dirk on the way. He did not answer, and so she left a message. She called Kathy and she didn't answer her phone either. She left another message., Texting is so much more efficient, Sarah thought. She arrived home to an excited Chloe. Sarah changed her clothes and got ready to go on her evening walk. Chloe dragged her to the front porch and started growling. Sarah saw the package.

"This is my lucky day. Two packages in the same day. I wonder who this is from." She opened the card, intending to take the package in after the walk. The card read, 'carpe diem, quam minimum credula postero.' That was odd. Why would someone leave that note, and not sign the card? Something was wrong. Sarah pulled out her phone.

Sarah: I got a bizarre note and a bottle of champagne on the front porch today. I am taking Chloe for a walk. Call you later. I hope you got that list of people.

Kathy: Busy interviewing families. Will call you. Under NO circumstances should you touch that bottle or open it! Understand!
Sarah: 🙁

She and Chloe headed off for their walk.

Call 911

Tim and Dave were back in the office after having gotten nowhere in Texas. Dave was sitting and talking to Dirk and Pat, in Dirk's office. "That guy Baronsky or whatever it is, he doesn't have a case. In fact, we should countersue, because we say the EYE BOT must be returned. We can't even find out where it is, let alone get it back."

Pat slapped Dave on the shoulder. "That, Dave is a great idea. I will start to work on the countersuit paperwork. I will pull the contract from Mrs Carmichael. The contract states that each BOT is worth over five hundred thousand dollars and if it is not returned, the individual or family will be billed for the entire amount. Do you know when it was online last?"

"No, Pat, I don't. But if you ask Tim, he will give you the dates. We keep track of that. If I remember correctly, it had gone offline before the incident and we were trying to find out then where it was. I wonder if the niece's information is in any of that paperwork. Will you let us know if you find any information on Caly Parker?"

Pat stood to leave. "Will do. I'll see you gentlemen later. I think this is a good approach. I still must send the rebuttal letter, but I will amend it with this threat of a countersuit. I am sure they are looking for much more than we are, but it won't matter. I doubt this will ever get to a courtroom for a judge or jury. I guess a lot will depend on whether the niece plays the role of victim. I can almost guarantee you, she will. Mr Baronsky will play on the sympathy of anyone listening to him."

"So, Dirk, what about your news? You found the girl? Tell me about it." Dave sat grinning, leaned forward and was making an out-with-it kind of motion.

"There is not much to tell. In fact, I botched it before I even got much of a chance with her. I already apologized and sent two dozen long stem roses."

Dave whistled, and wiped his forehead in a teasing way. "You must have done something really bad to have to send roses before you even get started."

"Starting at the beginning, she found me. Her name is Sarah; she is a researcher. We met for a drink. I am not sure, but I think she thought I called her fat, when I implied I thought she would order a salad for dinner. That is not what I meant, but that is how she took it, and I couldn't get my foot out of my mouth fast enough, or at all. She got up and left. The good news is, we have another date on Saturday. The roses did their magic. It works every time."

"Oh, is that your secret? I will remember that, if I ever have a date that I screw up before I get started," Dave teased. "Seriously, I am glad you found her. If you don't mind my saying, you were getting a little unbearable."

"I know; I am sorry about that. You are supposed to punch me when I get like that."

"I tried, but you punched back," replied Dave. He got up and pretended to punch Dirk in the stomach.

Dirk laughed. "I hear you. I will be better. I think we are on the right track with the BOT lawsuit. I also think I am going to marry Sarah."

"Whoa. You said you found her; you didn't say anything about marrying her."

"I know. But I just know. I fell in love the minute I looked into those eyes and she pulled me into her world. It is a place I never want to leave."

"Whoa, man, have you been reading romance novels or worse, watching romance TV? Who says that that stuff except for those men? They make it too hard for the rest of us to live up to the expectations those TV shows give women. Good luck." Dave headed into the staff room to see if there was anything to munch on. He found Gina sitting with a bottle of wine and some cheese and crackers. "What are you celebrating?"

"I was hungry. I found this in the fridge. I figure it is almost the end of the day. I opened it. You want a glass?"

"No thanks, I'll pass. I am not much for whites. I drive home; you can just walk. Did you hear that Dirk found the girl and then blew it?"

"He what?" Gina looked incredulous. "I find her, and he screws it up. Go figure."

"Wait, what do you mean, you found her?"

"I found her in the gym. I gave her the number to call Dirk. It took her long enough. What happened?"

"I think it had something to do with him calling her fat."

Gina laughed. "Well, she is fluffy. But he still shouldn't have called her that to her face."

"Gina, you are not nice, even if you did give her his number. Have a good night. I am tired. I am going home."

Gina was still sitting in the staff room well past the time when most of the office staff had gone home. She finished off the bottle of wine. Dirk was still finishing up paperwork. Pat was online, filing the countersuit. Gina was texting with China about meeting at the gym.

> Gina: Sorry China, I can't come to the gym tonight. I drunk a bottle of white.
> China: It sounds more like you are drunk. You okay to get home?
> Gina: Sure, I am, wait, I am going to toss my cookies. I'll get back to you.

China tried to call Gina, but Gina was sitting with her head in a trash can. She didn't answer. China headed out of her apartment toward the office to check on Gina. Gina fell to the floor in a heap. Pat heard a noise and ran

229

in to find her lying face down in her vomit. Pat gagged a little herself but recognized this was serious, so she tried not to look or do any breathing as she called for Dirk. Dirk did not answer. He was sitting in his chair with his head on his desk. He did not hear Pat's calls. Pat called 911.

"Operator, I'm — my — there is someone passed out and she doesn't answer when I shake her and call her name."

The 911 operator directed Pat. "Check to see if she is breathing. If she isn't, you are going to have to start CPR."

"I don't know how."

The 911 operator kept Pat on the phone; she gave her directions and helped to keep Pat calm. Pat went through the motions; it felt like forever until the paramedics were trying to get in the door. She buzzed to let them in.

China arrived at the front of the building at approximately the same time as the ambulance. China followed them to the BOT offices. She could not believe what she found upon arrival. Gina was on the floor and looked as pale as the wine she said she was drinking earlier, only her lips were as blue as blueberries. Pat was covered in puke and grabbed a paramedic and started pulling her down the hall. Tears ran down China's face as she stood staring at her best friend while the paramedics went to work.

After sending Dirk and Gina off in the ambulances, Pat called Dave and Greta to tell them the news. Dave and Greta were conferenced in and both were trying to talk, while Pat was trying to drive behind the ambulance. Relaying the story, the best way she could while concentrating on driving, Pat clenched the steering wheel and stepped on the gas to keep up.

"Let me just tell you the story before you ask too many questions that I don't know the answer to. I heard a thud and found Gina unresponsive and on the floor in the lunchroom. Gina wasn't breathing. I called 911. The 911 operator walked me through the steps to do CPR. I did that until the ambulance arrived. I took the paramedics to the staff kitchen to help Gina. I went to see if Dirk had gone home because he didn't respond to my calls for help. When I got to his office, I found him face down on his desk. His lips were blue too, but he was breathing. I ran to get a paramedic to take care of him. They called for another ambulance to come. The paramedics continued CPR on Gina and started giving oxygen to Dirk. Gina was breathing when they put her in the ambulance and the paramedic said she was stable. The paramedics asked me all kinds of questions. I had no idea how to respond. I told them that Gina and Dirk both ate the cheese and Gina drank the wine that came in a gift basket today. They asked if the rest of the staff had the cheese or the wine. I told them I had no idea. Gina and Dirk were loaded into the ambulances and the paramedics told me to meet them at Mercy Hospital.

Then I called you two. Oh, and Gina's friend China showed up. Apparently, texting her was the last thing Gina did before she threw up and passed out."

Dave and Greta asked Pat to stay at the hospital until they got there. Pat ran a red light after the ambulance. "Like I would think of being anywhere else. Hurry."

The director at Mercy Hospital was informed that two people were brought to the emergency department in critical condition. She was told that based on the information provided, they had food poisoning, or they were poisoned on purpose. The director shook her head. There had not been any cases in a couple of weeks. She had thought this was over.

A Public Health Problem

Kathy was at the food pantry early to meet with the director. She had the list of victims and was expecting to cross-reference it with the food pantry clients. She also intended to discuss discontinuing the distribution of the juices, or at least the ones that were listed as having high contents of arsenic.

"Hi, are you Donna, the director?"

Donna reached out to shake Kathy's hand. Kathy did the same.

"Yes, I am Donna. How can I help you, detective? I heard your message. It sounds dire."

"Please, call me Kathy. It is dire. I don't know how much you know about the products you distribute or if that falls to someone else. But you have a problem."

"Excuse me — we are careful to follow all of the out-of-dates printed on packaging, we get our food from reputable sources and we don't give out anything that is damaged or opened. What do you mean we have a problem? We have not broken any laws. We work with the health department to make sure that we are complying in every way. I assure you."

"Slow down and take a deep breath. I promise you — I don't think you have done anything wrong or broken any laws. One of the manufacturers of juices that you distribute is pushing the gray area of the law. One of your clients, a Mr Daniel King, is dead, and his wife is having what we believe to be side effects of arsenic poisoning."

Donna gasped and plopped down on the closest chair. She was pasty white and turning green; she looked like someone who was about to throw up breakfast.

"Oh no," she cried, "I know them personally. I don't know all our clients, but they are some of my very favorites. They volunteer here regularly. I wondered where they have been. How, where, when…?"

Kathy stopped the questions by interrupting Donna and went on with the story.

"Mr King died a few weeks ago. He was admitted to the hospital with symptoms of the flu. He died of heart failure. I saw his wife a couple of days ago. She is not good. She probably didn't contact you because she doesn't believe that her husband is dead. I contacted her son and she is possibly in the hospital today being treated."

"Oh, this is awful. What do you mean the juices have arsenic in them?"

"That is a long story. I need you to stop distributing any apple or grape juice of any kind until I can work through all the details with you. I am working with someone who will help you understand what is going on and be able to figure out what you should do next. Her name is Sarah. I'll get her to call you and set up an appointment. In the meantime, I need the records of all your clients. I need to cross- reference their names with the twenty-six people I have on a list."

Donna looked hesitant. "Is it okay for me to share them with you? We have a strict privacy policy here. But it seems important for you to know if those twenty-six people got juice from us."

"That's what I need. Do you have a tech person who can take my list and cross-reference it with your clients? Then I don't need access to your files."

"Can you give me a couple of hours? I will have someone here do that for you. I am sure you have more important things to do than cross-checking lists. Can you tell me what hospital Mrs King is in? I would like to see her."

"I do not know. I will have that information for you when we speak again. Here is my list. Thank you for your cooperation. I will check back with you after lunch. Thank you for your time. See you later."

Kathy turned to leave and pondered her next actions in this very weird case. She checked her phone and saw the earlier text from Sarah. That is where she would go next.

Kathy: Hey, where are you? Where is that bottle of champagne?

Kathy headed to her car. By the time she was sitting behind the wheel, her phone buzzed.

Sarah: I am home. The bottle is on the porch. Are you coming over?
Kathy: Yes, I am headed that way. BRT

Sarah was staring at the flowers from Dirk and imagining their upcoming date. The flowers really were extraordinary. It was kind of him to apologize. It was the first time a man had admitted to his bad behavior, by sending this many flowers. He was handsome and funny, and Sarah was smitten. She turned back to her computer, continuing to look for a colorless, odorless and water-soluble chemical that could be used for a poison. Arsenic had been the poison of choice for every maniac murderer in every detective show on TV and in the movies since 'Arsenic and Old Lace' opened on Broadway in 1941. The other popular choices were either insulin, or digitalis which came from the plant foxglove. Unfortunately, murders in real life were also executed with these same poisons, and others. Each of these drugs was used in the hope that it wouldn't be discovered by medical professionals and they were somewhat easy to obtain if one knew what to get. Insulin was available without a prescription at any local pharmacy. Sarah continued noodling around what the other options might be. What was the method that this murderer was using? It seemed it would be hard to get twenty-six people to drink something unless it was at a party or a cult gathering. That could not be the case here as all these individuals were admitted weeks or months apart. There was a knock at the door. Sarah jumped, and Chloe barked, 'woof'. Sarah got up from her seat and went to the door. She peeked to see who it was. It was Kathy. Sarah calmed Chloe and opened the door. Kathy had on gloves and the bottle of champagne in her hand. Chloe started barking wildly at the bottle.

Kathy asked, "Is this the bottle? It seems Chloe doesn't like something about it."

"Good afternoon to you too. That is the bottle. It is Chloe that showed me that it was on the porch. I never use that door. She can see out the sidelight. If she could talk, she could tell us who dropped it by. Look at this note." Sarah got the note and handed it to Kathy. "This was with it," said Sarah. "I have 'Carpe diem' in my signature line for my emails. But I don't have the whole quote."

Kathy read, "Carpe diem, quam minimum credula postero."

Sarah hesitated before saying, "Is this the part where it is getting dangerous?"

Kathy looked at her and took off her sunglasses. "I don't think this has anything to do with the murders. If I must bet, I'd say this is your girl from class. I don't think she wants to celebrate with you. I'd say there is poison in this bottle, and she intends to celebrate your leaving the university in a box."

Chills ran down Sarah's spine.

Chloe voiced 'woof'.

"I am taking this to the lab. Any suggestions for what the technician should look for in it?"

"I am just researching that very thing. Well, not what is in the bottle, but what kind of chemicals might be suspect in this case. I wish we could find some common thread, but I don't know if that will make it easier or harder. I am not answering your question, because I don't know the answer. Let's sit down and have something to drink. I can fill you in on what I have been thinking. You can fill me in on the list."

Sarah made some iced tea and set some cookies on the table. She gave Chloe a treat. The women sat down at the table.

Sarah, with a cookie in hand, pointed at Kathy. "Spill."

Kathy laughed. "Can't a girl get a drink and a cookie first? I went to the food pantry this morning. They are cross-checking our list of twenty-six with their clients. Donna the director was sad when I told her about the Kings. She said that they volunteer there. That reminds me. Have you heard from Jeff King about his mother?"

"Yes, he called me to tell me that she is in Baptist Hospital. There really is not a treatment for arsenic poisoning but they are giving her fluids to hydrate her. He will get someone to stay with her until she recovers. She is older so it may take a while. How well she

238

recovers will depend on how much damage has been done by the arsenic."

"I told Donna I would be back to pick up the list after lunch. Do you have class this afternoon? We can drop the champagne off at the lab and go pick up the list and then start working on it. I also told Donna you will work with her on what to do about the juices, and maybe you should think about a plan to check on everyone who has been getting the juice."

"I am done with class for the day. Oh, that reminds me. See those lovely red roses? Those are from Dirk. I'll get my bag. Are we taking Chloe?"

"Very nice flowers. I guess he wants to make up for the other night. Let's leave Chloe home for now to guard the house."

Thallium, Is it?

Sarah and Kathy headed for the food pantry to pick up the list. Donna was waiting when they arrived with the names that had been matched to their clients.

"Thank you, Donna, this is helpful. Let me introduce you to Doctor Sarah Sandling. She offered to help you with the juice disaster."

Donna looked at Sarah. "Oh, you are a physician?"

Sarah responded, "No, I study medicinal plants and I am a pharmacist. I understand you also want to know about Mrs King. She is in Baptist Hospital. Her son is with her. I am sure she will enjoy a visit from you. Now, tell me when a good time for us to get together and plan will be. I think we need to take all the juice off the shelves for now, and we need to send anyone who has been getting the juices to their doctors for heavy metal testing. Adults and children included, especially the children." Sarah paused and weighed what she had just said and gave Donna a minute to process. "Wait, I might see if I can set up a clinic here with the county, so let me check into that before you contact people and scare them. I will call you later this afternoon. Is that okay?"

Donna's head was spinning. "Yes, of course. I think I need some time to think about all that you have said."

Kathy said with a grin, "Sometimes talking to Sarah is like having a fire hose turned on full blast and pointed at you. You'll get used to it."

Donna smiled, and sighed beneath her breath. "I sincerely doubt it."

Kathy laughed. "We need to be going now. We'll be back in touch."

The women took their leave and headed toward the door.

Sarah looked at Kathy. "Is that what you think? I am like a fire hose? I think you need to send me two dozen long-stemmed roses for that remark."

Kathy laughed. "Don't hold your breath."

The women headed back to the DSA with the list.

Sarah said, "I was online doing more research for poisons. I was thinking about the heavy metal testing that Doctor Canon did. There are a couple of metals that might have potential that he did not test for; one is thallium. There is an optics company close to the university. Thallium is used in the creation and development of some types of lenses for glasses. It is also used in nuclear medicine. That means there is a potential supply in the area. Chromium is another option, but I don't think that is a viable one. I found a case online where a woman killed her husband using thallium."

"Of course you did," said Kathy, rolling her eyes as she grinned, waiting for a response from her sidekick.

"I am serious. It's as good as anything you have produced. I just can't come up with a plant poison that has the same symptoms and kills after chronic use rather than immediately. I know there must be some. I just can't think of them, and when I do come up with a name, there is no way to test for it. Those kinds of poisons just make normal body functions go crazy and that's why people die. It is why people use them for murder. No one can tell, and they get away with it, like now."

"Hold on. No one is getting away with anything. We are going to find out what is happening. We have already determined that several deaths were not murders. That should make you happy."

"It would if it weren't for the fact that in almost all of the cases, the deaths might have been prevented. That makes me sad."

Kathy pulled into the parking lot of the DSA. "We are here; let's take the bottle to the lab, and get it dusted for fingerprints. I don't think we will find any, but just in case." Sarah got out of the car and walked with Kathy into the building. Kathy handed the bottle to the lab technician. "Test this for any kind of contaminant you can think of. If you can test for it, run it, and that includes thallium."

The lab technician took the bottle carefully from Kathy. "Thallium isn't such an easy test to run. It might take me a couple days. There are only a few labs that run that test. I'll get to work on searching for every other contaminant, detective. I'll keep you posted as the results come back."

"Thank you. Come on Sarah, let's go look at that list."

Sarah and Kathy had the lists spread out on the conference room table. Sarah went through them and compared.

"Kathy, look at this. They have fifteen people on the list that match ours. Did you ask her to sort out the people who got juice from people who did not? If you didn't then I don't know if we can automatically say that all these people died from arsenic poisoning."

"No, I just asked her to tell me who on her client list matched the twenty-six people on ours. Do you think they even keep track of what food they distribute to whom?"

Sarah shook her head. "I have no idea. Maybe not — that is a specific detail. Back to the drawing board. Let me think."

"I'll call to see if they keep a list of what they give to people."

"Before you do that, didn't Doctor Canon say he tested everyone after Mr King for arsenic?

"I think he did. Let's look at the hospital and autopsy labs on just those fifteen people from the food pantry and see who has a level of arsenic reported."

Sarah worked through the lists. Kathy looked through her emails to see if there were any leads. She found none. She went back to the files to see if there were any clues that she was missing.

"Sarah, are you getting anywhere?"

"I have a couple more names at least: Haley Mills and Delanor Green are the two after Mr King that have arsenic levels reported. There are some names on here before Mr King died that are on both the lists and they did not have heavy metal toxicity screens done. If I add the five people who likely had the flu, and the three people who had arsenic levels reported, then that leaves us with eighteen people or less who might have been murdered. Maybe we can find something in common among them. Let's see if any of them lived in the same facility as my mom's friend Ruth. Can you call that director and get a list, or give them our list for a comparison?"

Just as Sarah mentioned her mother's name, her phone rang with 'Mamma Mia'. Kathy laughed. Sarah looked at Kathy. "How does she know?"

Kathy was still laughing at the ringtone. "How does who, know what?"

"I just mentioned my mom and I have a text from her. How does she do that?"

"That is your mother's ringtone," asked Kathy.

Sarah nodded.

Kathy laughed, shrugged, and went back to the files. Sarah unlocked the phone to get the text.

Mom: Sarah, this is mom. I haven't heard from you. Are you busy?

Sarah: you don't have to tell me it's you. I can tell from the phone number. Yes, I am busy. Is everything okay with you and daddy?

Mom: Yes, we are fine. Why don't you and Chloe come to dinner tonight?

Sarah: Let me see mom, I'll get back to you.

"Kathy, do you want to go to dinner at my mom's tonight?"

Kathy looked up from the files. "Sure, a girl has to eat. You need someone to make sure you don't get into trouble."

Sarah: I will be there at six with Chloe and my girlfriend Kathy.

"I'll put in a call to the director where Ruth Morgan lived." Kathy picked up the phone and punched in the number.

Corina's Discovery

Corina was in the MassageMe office with Tracy. Tracy created the list of names of people who had not been back and associated the names with the therapist they saw most often, although not exclusively. She also included the last time they were in for a massage. She gave it to Corina. Corina took the list and began reviewing it.

"This person's name is really Astral Moon?"

"I know, I tried not to giggle every time she came in for a massage. I liked her. She always told me my horoscope for the day."

Corina made a face and said, "Ay, dios mio, you are kidding right?"

"No, I am not. I noticed that there are one or two therapists listed most. I know people do not like Charleen. They try not to rebook her. Sometimes there isn't a choice when the person from that retirement community calls to schedule the appointments. Only one or two of the people on that list liked her enough to go back more than three times and then they didn't come back, or they switched to another therapist."

"Tracy, Es muy importante que no le digas a nadie que hiciste esta lista. ¿Entiendes?"

"Corina. I am not telling anyone that I made that list." Tracy got up to leave and looked back at Corina. "What are you going to do now?"

Corina looked back at Tracy, bewildered. "No tengo ni idea. I really have no idea. I don't know what it means. Just please keep it quiet."

Tracy shook her head and left the office.

Corina stared at the list, wondering what it meant. She thought, this wasn't very many people, they were most all from one retirement community, but not everyone. Maybe they just decided they did not want massages any more. What did this list mean? She put the list in the drawer and locked it. Then she left the office.

Martha Bright — Pinter 11 months
Hannah Overman — Parker 11 months
Carmine Windsor- — Parker 11 months
Hallie Vincent — Pinter 10 months
Jenny Crane — Pinter 10 months
Hortense Appleton — Parker 9 months
Layla Merton — Parker 9 months
Opal Wright — Pinter 8 months
Darnell Miller — Smith 10 months
Sarah West — Parker 7 months
Kim Teller — Parker 7 months
Astral Moon — Smith 6 months
Barbara Grant — Parker 6 months
Sheila Cray — Smith 5 months

Samantha Cook — Pinter 4 months
Delia Brach — Parker 3 months
Jules Verne — Pinter 3 months
Lina Mount — Graham 2 months
Lola Reed — Parker 1 month
Cristine Poe — Parker 1 month
Ruth Morgan — Parker 3 weeks

Charleen was coming out of a room when she ran into Harold. She did not even see him as she was concentrating on other events in her life. She looked up. "Oh Harold, excuse me. I was thinking about something else."

Harold gently took a hold of her arm. "Good afternoon, Charleen. I was thinking of something too — you." He grinned.

Charleen looked around nervously. "I really need to get back into the room. I just stepped out for my client to get ready. Maybe we can talk later." She went back into the room, leaving Harold in the hallway wondering what just happened.

Women, he thought. I will never understand them. Harold was busy all afternoon and didn't see Charleen again for most of the shift. He went looking for Corina to discuss operations in the office.

Tracy told Harold, "She is out for a little while. She said she will be back this evening. She is going to stay late tonight."

Harold tried to hide his distress. "Did she say how late, or why? She usually goes home early."

"I don't know, Harold, but she seems much more interested in the company than she has for a while."

Harold looked at Tracy, puzzled. "Why do you say that?"

Tracy tried to maintain a poker face. "No reason. She just seems to be paying more attention. That's all I meant."

Harold turned to walk back to the staff office. "Please let me know when my next appointment is here. I am going to eat my meal. Thank you."

Harold got to the staff office and prepared his food but was not paying attention. He was focused on what he was going to do if he could not spend time with Charleen. Number one, she seemed upset and maybe they needed to talk, not to be intimate. He felt the rise in his scrubs the minute he began to imagine Charleen in a negligee. He continued to ponder and to determine the best way forward for the evening if Corina was staying until close. He and Charleen might have to go to the bar or somewhere else. Maybe to Charleen's place. He continued to plan while he ate his meal and then got ready for the next client. There was still no sign of Charleen.

Charleen was in a bad mood. She had been in a sour mood since she received the letter. She had been sure that she would receive a check. Things were not going her way these days. The only good thing in her life was

Harold. When she evaluated everything in her life, she realized that even the relationship with him would not be able to go on forever. Her girlfriends warned her that it was impossibly complicated to get involved with a married man. She tried to explain that he had given her a gift, no matter what happened in the future. She was free from her mother's prudish attitude toward sex. Her family treated her poorly, and her father used to sneak into her room at night. When she told her mother, her mother just blamed Charleen. Years of therapy did not free her the way her affair with Harold had. She was afraid he would let her down too, like all the others. She finished the massage for the client and left the room. She ran into Corina. It was nine p.m. Charleen thought to herself, what is she doing here at this time of night?

She stopped to ask. "Corina, it's late. I don't usually see you at this time of night."

Corina smiled. "Hello. I think it is good to be here at night sometimes. I understand the girls at the front desk have been leaving the therapists alone to go home and study. I am just making sure that everything is operating as it should. Do you need anything, Charleen? Is everything okay? You seem perturbed?"

"I am not perturbed. I have been concentrating and giving massages for the last eight hours. I am tired. I have one more hour massage. Will you be here at ten when I am finished?"

Corina looked at her watch. She told Charleen she was committed to closing the office. Charleen sighed and walked to the staff office for a drink before the last client. She really hoped that she and Harold would be able to talk and maybe have a little fun after work. Now, she devised a plan. She wondered, would Harold be willing to go to her place?

She quickly wrote a note with her address and directions to the condo. Charleen walked to the hallway to see if Harold was between clients. She saw him standing in front of room four. She walked down the hall and slipped the note into his pocket and continued walking to greet her next client.

Harold read the note. 'My love, it seems that we will not be able to meet in our usual place tonight. Here is my address. Please come over around 10.30. I will be waiting impatiently to wrap my arms and lips around you. Are you up for it? So to speak. XOXO.'

Harold was stunned. He had been sure that he would be going straight home tonight. He thought to himself, if I go to her home, will she think I intend to leave Mary? He could not leave Mary, but he couldn't stop making love to Charleen. What was he going to do? He felt himself getting hard while he pondered the predicament he was in. The excitement of the secret affair had given him new life. He was torn. He turned and went into the room to finish the evening's work before he decided what he would do. Even though he already knew.

Corina turned on the alarm and locked the doors to the MassageMe. She walked out of the door with the therapists. She wondered about Harold and Charleen. She was sure that something was going on between them, but there was nothing unusual that she could identify tonight. They walked to their separate cars after saying polite good nights.

She thought to herself, maybe I am wrong. But she didn't think so.

And So it Goes

Harold arrived at the condo just a little ahead of ten thirty. It was far enough from his home that he believed that no one who knew Mary would be around to recognize him. He was thankful that he no longer lived in Euclid. Everyone knew all your business there. He felt he was much more suited to this city. He took the flowers that he stopped to buy out of the car and headed to the door. Charleen answered and pulled him inside. She wrapped her arms around him and planted a kiss on his lips that he was sure would be his undoing. He dropped the bouquet and wrapped both arms around her. He kissed her back. He pulled her to the sofa, and they fell together laughing. Charleen was struggling to remove her shirt through the kiss. Harold stopped them.

"Charleen, I want to talk first."

Charleen looked surprised. "Well, that's a first. A man who wants to talk before having sex. Usually that is after the deed is done, along with a cigarette."

"Charleen, please, I am being serious. You seemed upset tonight at the office. I feel like something is bothering you. Can we talk about it? Also, we need to figure out why Corina suddenly has an interest in staying at night."

Charleen laid her hand on his chest and started a massage. Harold was slowly forgetting that he wanted to talk. Charleen softly kissed his neck. "Harold, there are many important things we should talk about. There is nothing that I want to talk about now. I want you to take the vibrator that is sitting on the table and use it in all the right places. I want to scream your name in passion when I come. I want to find new positions tonight that we cannot do on a massage table. I want you to make love to me, not talk."

"Your wish is my command. Hand over that vibrator."

Harold took the vibrator and turned it on. He placed it between her legs on the outside of her clothing. She sucked in a breath and sighed. Harold wrapped his other arm around her and pulled her close. He suggested they move to a more comfortable place to try out those new positions. By the time they had moved to the bedroom, Charleen was in her lingerie and Harold had nothing on but his manhood. Harold took her breasts in his hands. He played with her nipples over her bra. He nipped until they were hard, and he played with them through the sheer material. He liked to tease them to the point that Charleen moaned with delight. Charleen was lying back and enjoying the feeling that Harold gave her when they were together like this. Then he moved over her and placed the vibrator between her legs. She arched into him and worked to take off her panties. Harold obliged and helped her remove them and her bra. He rubbed the toy against her. Then he moved down her body with his lips, kissed her and licked until she was begging him to let her return the favor. He sucked a little and looked to see Charleen's expression. She was smiling and looking at him in a way that no one ever had before. He belonged here in this moment, with her. He knew that to his core. Yet, there was something that he couldn't quite reach at the edge of his thoughts, but he was taken back to the moment before he could find it. He licked and fondled her until he could tell she was almost ready to come. Then he moved his lips back up to her breasts.

"I think, these need some more attention before we move on to a new position. What do you think?"

"Forget new positions."

"Oh no, you asked, and we are going to keep you in suspense a little longer."

Charleen moaned and had no choice but to give in. Harold continued to use the vibrator on the lowest speed. He rolled her over and inserted the vibrator slowly and turned up the speed. He continued to tease until he could no longer control his own feelings. He replaced the vibrator with his own hot hard flesh. Charleen let out a wildly erotic scream with his name on her lips. Harold came with that sound and filled Charleen until he felt her second orgasm. He was almost spent but made one more thrust until they both came one more time.

Harold woke to the sound of his phone.

Mary: Where are you?

Crap, was it really five a.m.?

He hung his head wondering what to do. He turned off the phone and rolled over, waking Charleen before he had to go. He kissed her mouth and played with her tongue until she was kissing him back.

"It's five a.m. I need to go."

Charleen looked at him through sleep-fogged eyes. "Please don't."

"I am sorry. I must go."

"Parting is such sweet sorrow," whispered Charleen.

"What?"

Charleen rolled over on her side. "Nothing. I'll see you at work. Thank you."

Harold leaned back over her and nuzzled her neck. He kissed her one parting kiss.

Charleen watched him walk out the door and heard the front door close. She let her thoughts wander to the night before and rolled back over to sleep.

"Goodbye Harold Pinter. I love you."

Harold headed toward home. He needed a shower, he needed a coffee and he needed some relief for the hard-on he had because he was not ready to leave Charleen. What was he going to do? Mary would be awake. He couldn't go home to her like this. He pulled out his phone, turned it back on and received three more texts, all from Mary.

Harold: Mary, I am fine. I am sorry I worried you. I went out with the guys and got a little too drunk to drive home. I am at their place and was sleeping it off. My phone was off. I'll drop by the office and see you later this morning. Love you.

Harold sighed and rubbed his chin. Could he go back to Charleen's place?

He rejected the idea and turned the car around and headed for the truck stop on I-75, even though it was in the opposite direction from home. It seemed he was destined to go in the opposite direction of home from now on, because of the choice he had made to love Charleen.

He wondered for the first time — could he leave Mary?

Mercy Hospital

The staff arriving at the BOT Inc. offices in the morning entered to find Greta and Dave looking anxious and exhausted. Dave herded the entire staff to the conference room and asked them to take a seat. He provided the best information he could on the status of Dirk and Gina and how it came to be that they were admitted to the hospital the night before. There were questions, such as would they be all right. Dave shrugged his shoulders. "I hope so. The physicians do not know what is wrong; they are working under a hypothesis that the two were poisoned. They are running tests. Both are in the intensive care unit and being supported with a respirator." He sighed, continuing on. "You cannot go visit them at this time. We will keep you all posted. In the meantime, everyone can take the day off. I know this comes as a shock to you all."

The staff slowly left the conference room, whispering among themselves. Some headed out the door to work from home. Tim stayed in the office, along with Jessie Smith, the assistant at the front desk who took the basket from the delivery man.

Greta looked at Dave. "Do you think I should throw all the food away, or do you think there is some reason to keep it?"

"I don't know. But do not let anyone else eat it. Keep the wine bottle in case the physicians are correct. The police will want it. I don't believe that Gina drank herself sick. She has a high tolerance for her liquor. Where did that basket come from?"

Greta got the card for Dave and told him that there wasn't even a delivery company name on the card or box.

Dave read the card and asked, "Did Dirk see this?"

Greta replied fretfully, "Yes, I showed it to him. He didn't seem to think anything of it. We laughed that it seemed ominous. I guess it wasn't funny. He didn't know who sent it. You know, Jessie might know something. She called me and said that the delivery man specifically said this was for Dirk. He always shares and so I just brought it into the staff office. Should we be calling the police, or will they do that at the hospital?"

Dave looked at Greta. "And what will we tell them?"

"Well, it seems we have a lot to tell them, Dave. Things like this happen on TV and they always call the police."

"Of course they do." Dave slumped into a chair sighing heavily. He was tired, his best friend was in the hospital and the assistant was talking about crime TV. He thought, this was why people drank in the morning.

Dave looked up at Greta. "Yes, I believe you need to call the police. We probably should have done that last night. I'll be in the office; let me know when they arrive."

Greta placed the call. She was told that the homicide police officers were on the way. They were called by an administrator at Mercy Hospital early this morning and had already begun their investigation.

In the meantime, Dave called Pat to get an update on his friends. Pat relayed that nothing had changed since they talked last and she told him the police were there earlier. Pat asked about calling Dirk and Gina's families. Dave said he would call Dirk's family, and that she should call Gina's mother. Gina's father had passed away when she was a little girl.

Dave hung up. This was not a phone call any mother wanted to get. What would he say?

The police detectives arrived at the BOT offices about a half-hour later. Greta let them in and took them to show them the staff lunchroom and then to Dirk's office. There were two detectives from the Miami-Dade County sheriff's office. The officers roped off the staff lunchroom with caution tape and no one was allowed in or out. They took the wine bottle and the cheese pieces that were left and put them in an evidence bag to take away with them. Greta called Dave to join them in Dirk's office. Dave arrived and everyone took a seat. The officers began with questions about what happened and moved on to theories. They wanted to know if Greta or Dave had an idea about who would want to harm Dirk or Gina. Neither could come up with a reason or a person. They told the officers that the basket was delivered to Dirk, but Greta put it in the staff office because Dirk always shared those kinds of gifts.

Greta asked, "Is there something else we should be doing? Do you want to dust the card for fingerprints?"

The lead officer responded, "I don't think we want to dust it for prints, because now several people have touched it, but I would like to see it and keep it with the evidence."

Greta went with one of the officers to get the card.

Dave was shaking his head in anguish. "How does this kind of stuff happen?"

"Sir, we live in Miami-Dade County, where anything is possible. The criminals here are like nowhere else. I think it's the Everglades."

"Excuse me; what do the Everglades have to do with it?"

The officer smiled. "Because their cosmic influence on the locals is undeniable."

Dave just shook his head, thinking there must be close to three thousand officers in Miami-Dade County and I get the nut job.

The officers spoke with Jessica for a couple of minutes and then took their leave with instructions to Greta and Dave to keep them informed of the status of the victims. Dave walked to his office and found Tim working at his desk. "Tim, I told everyone to go home. Why are you still here?"

"Well, Doctor Johnson, I know that Doctor Keene is your best friend and that you care very much for Ms Portense, even if she is kind of hard to get along with. I thought you might need someone to talk to. Plus, I think you should go home. So, I stayed to tell you that."

"Tim, that is kind of you. I do not feel like talking. I really want to find that niece and the EYE BOT that was Betty Carmichael's. I want to be at the hospital, and I want to sleep. The problem is, I am not sure which order to put those things in now."

"I can tell you. You need to sleep. I'll work on finding Caly Parker. Go home; that's an order."

Dave looked at Tim and laughed. "You are not the boss of me."

They both laughed at the inside joke and Dave began to cry. "What if something happens to Dirk? We have been together most of our lives. I care for Gina; I don't want to lose her. You are right; I need to get some sleep. Thank you and I'll check in with you later."

"I'll take care of the office. I'll talk to Jessie and we will answer phones today and keep the press at bay. I suspect at some point they will be showing up. Someone is going to leak this to the news media."

Dave looked at Tim, surprised. "Ugh, I hadn't even thought of that. Thank you."

Dave stopped by Dirk's office on the way out to see if his phone was there. He found it lying on the desk, picked it up, turned it off, and put it in his pocket. Then he stopped by Gina's office to get her phone and any other personal items that shouldn't be lying around the office. He left the BOT offices headed for home and a shower, and a trip back to the hospital to relieve Pat.

Charleen Makes Nice

Kathy had told Sarah at dinner the night before that she should start taking Chloe with her to school. This morning Sarah was debating whether that was a good idea. There wasn't a policy against pets at the school, but she wasn't sure there was one that allowed pets to be on campus if they weren't service dogs. She took Chloe for a walk and decided to leave her at home. Kathy was being overprotective. Sarah headed out the door for the food bank, and school.

She told Chloe, "Guard the house."

Sarah: Kathy I am on my way to the food bank. Anything we need from them? Did you get a hold of the director at the assisted living facility where Ruth lived?

Sarah also sent a text to Donna to say she would stop by the offices that morning to discuss what to do about the juices and the people who might have been drinking them. Before she could start the car and move out into traffic, her phone buzzed.

Kathy: I am headed there now. I will let you know what I find out. Want to meet at the gym later?
Sarah: Sure, the gym it is, after that meal mom made, I definitely need to work out. C U L8R at 6?

Sarah: Dirk, I am looking forward to seeing you this evening. Where and when are we meeting. I am going to the gym at 6. What about 8, maybe somewhere on Brickell by your offices?

Sarah made the quick stop to see Donna. They determined that there needed to be a coordinated effort to contact everyone who had been drinking the juices from the companies that had high contents of arsenic. The staff at the health department weren't any help with setting up a clinic, because they were dealing with another H1N1 virus outbreak, which might have caused some of the deaths. The next best thing would be to call everyone. Donna indicated to Sarah that her staff would organize all their efforts toward notifying people. Donna promised to get everyone called before the end of the next day. She assured Sarah that they would start with the families who had children.

"I will create a letter for everyone to take to their physicians and email it to you by the end of the day," said Sarah. "Hopefully, you can get the letter into their hands before they go to their physician."

"No problem, Doctor Sandling. We will make sure we do."

Sarah asked Donna for one more favor before leaving. "I have finished going through the records from the hospital and the list that you supplied. I tried to make an educated guess about who might have been getting juices from the pantry. Can you tell me if these four people are on the food pantry list of people who get juices?"

Donna took a quick look and pulled out her list. It turned out that Sarah was correct. Darnell Miller, Livia Olds, Haley Mills and Delanor Green were all clients of the food pantry and liked to get juices.

Sarah left Donna with a promise to follow up quickly.

She headed to her car, thinking okay, that's a total of seven people who probably died from the flu and/or arsenic. If she added that to the people who died or likely died from influenza, that was five more people for a total of twelve. That means there were about fourteen whom they didn't know what happened to. That didn't make her feel better.

She got in the car and headed for school. She parked and was heading into the building just as the rain started and she got soaked. Oh great, she thought. I am already running late and now I look like a drowned rat. She needed to get that letter written for Donna and get some more research done in addition to preparing for class. She stopped quickly by her office to dry off, looked at her watch and realized she had time to text Kathy.

Sarah: I found four people who got juice from the food pantry. That leaves fourteen to figure out. Get anywhere on your end?

Sarah headed to class. Everyone was there, including Charleen who raised her eyebrows and lowered her eyes when Sarah looked in her direction.

"Good morning, everyone. I hope that you all had a great weekend and a chance to read the chapters on drug development. Charleen, why don't you give us a synopsis of the chapters. I am sure you read them since this is the area you are specifically interested in studying."

Charleen looked surprised. "Sure." She led a discussion with the rest of the students on drug development and in Sarah's opinion, did a good job.

Sarah guessed that her little talk with the chair had motivated her. When that discussion died down, Gary spoke up.

"Doctor Sandling, did you ever figure out the murder?"

Sarah thought, how do they know? Then she remembered she told them she was writing a book. She recovered quickly. "I did figure out who did it. But if I tell you, then you won't need to buy the book to find out." The class laughed, all but Charleen. She must still be angry, Sarah thought. She dismissed the class with instructions for the week's lab work. Everyone headed out, but Charleen stayed seated. Sarah gathered up her things as Charleen finally got up and approached her. Sarah stopped and looked at Charleen, waiting for her to say whatever it was that she was going to say.

Charleen asked, "How is your dog?"

Sarah thought, that is the strangest question from someone who said she was going to get me fired. She regained her composure. "Did I mention that I have a dog, Charleen? Chloe is fine. Are you an animal lover?"

"Yes, I am. I owe you an apology, Doctor Sandling. I was out of line the other day. I hope you will accept my apology."

"Thank you, Charleen. I appreciate that. I know that everyone has bad days. Is there something that I can do to help you get through this course? I think you did a good job leading the discussion today."

"No, I just wanted to make sure that we are okay. I know that I pushed the envelope of professional behavior in your office the other day. I have a lot going on." Charleen adopted a sickeningly sweet voice and politely added, "I'd like to make it up to you."

Sarah was suspicious at this point but maintained her light mood. "Charleen, thank you. That is all I needed. I do not hold grudges. I apologize but I must run. Is there more that we need to discuss? I'll be glad to set up an appointment for tomorrow morning."

"No, that is all I had to say." Charleen turned and headed out the door.

Sarah heard someone yell, "Hey, Caly, do you want to join us?" She wondered — who is Caly?

Sarah headed back to her office. She plopped in her chair and considered how strange that interaction was with Charleen. She unlocked her computer and the screen from her search on thallium came alive. She looked at her phone to see if anyone had sent her a text. Nothing from Kathy. Nothing from Dirk. She wondered if he was going to stand her up. She thought, that would be odd after he sent her all those roses. She went back to the computer screen and concentrated on creating the letter that Donna needed to give to all the clients from the food pantry. Sarah's phone beeped and she looked to see a notification from Kathy.

Kathy: Yes, 6 pm. See you then. Yes, I have a list to bring with me.

"Well that's one down." Sarah's phone played 'Mamma Mia'. She looked to see what her mother had to say.

Mom: Sarah, honey, it's mom. I just wanted to tell you how much your father and I enjoyed your friend Kathy joining us last night. I don't think you ate enough. Are you feeling all right?
Sarah: Mom, really? Love you, talk to you later.

Sarah finished the letter, and did some more searches on thallium and some plants that she thought had potential in this case. She had just enough time to go and take Chloe for a walk before heading to the gym. She didn't really worry about Chloe because she had a dog door that worked with a magnetic collar, but the yard was so small Sarah felt guilty if she did not give her a walk twice a day. Besides, it was easier than playing tug with her for an hour. Sarah got home and changed into the appropriate walking attire. Chloe was ready to go. They headed out for a short walk; as they passed the backyard window on the way out the door, Sarah noticed something that seemed out of place behind the gate. They took a detour through the backyard. There was a bag of dog food that had been dropped over the fence. It was lying open. Chloe sniffed, and started barking at Sarah. Sarah thought, this is so odd. She wondered why it was here. She wondered if Chloe had eaten any. She would eat cat poop; she had probably eaten some of this. Why was she barking at it?

Sarah left the bag for now and took Chloe into the house. She took the electric collar off so Chloe could not get to the backyard until Sarah cleaned up the food. They headed out the door for a quick walk. Then she headed to the gym.

Kathy and Sarah arrived at the gym about the same time. They headed to the usual spot for working out and Sarah told Kathy about her day. She started briefly describing the strange conversation with Charleen.

270

Then she told Kathy she was not going out with Dirk. Sarah did not understand why, after he sent all those roses and asked to go out last night, he didn't text her today. The women spent some time discussing the foibles of the modern man, from Sarah's perspective, and grabbed their equipment to work out.

"There are several people who lived at the same assisted living community as Ruth Morgan that are on our list of deceased individuals," said Kathy.

"That's awful. I hope we can figure this out soon."

"Well, maybe we can start to find a common thread. It looks like it's a good portion of the fourteen that you say are left that have been murdered."

Kathy and Sarah finished their workout and headed into the locker room.

Sarah cleaned up and asked, "Can we go sit somewhere quietly to talk about the commonalities of the people who are left on the list?"

Once they were seated, Sarah checked one more time for a text from Dirk. There was no text. "I was sure that he was sincere. I mean, who sends that kind of apology and doesn't follow through."

"Maybe something happened, and he just didn't get the opportunity to tell you. I think you need to cut the guy some slack."

"I want to, but he better be laying in a hospital bed knocked out for me to consider it."

Kathy laughed. "I think that is a little extreme. You will hear from him. Give him a chance."

Sarah paused thoughtfully. "Okay, what about the list? What questions did you ask the director about their activities, or diets? Does the cook there wash his hands? Maybe they got salmonella, got dehydrated and their potassium was high due to that."

"I don't think so. The coroner mentioned many of the people had the same kind of fingernail bed discoloration or lines. That points to all of them being poisoned with arsenic. The fact is though, the tests didn't come back positive for arsenic in these people that were not on the food pantry list. Did you find something else that changes nail bed coloration and causes high potassium?"

"Maybe — I am still thinking thallium. It's odorless, colorless and tasteless. It can be absorbed through the skin. In a high enough dose, it can be toxic quickly. In a low dose it would take time and it does cause nail bed changes. Did you get any information back from the lab on the bottle of champagne that was in front of my house? If you think someone is trying to poison me then they might be using the same chemical used on the other dead people on our list. Very weird things are happening. Today, there was a bag of dog food dumped over my fence and it was open lying on the ground. Chloe might have eaten some. I don't know. She seems fine. If she ate any, she didn't eat a lot, but I am going to watch her."

Kathy looked concerned. "I will want to take that food to the lab too. Let's go to your house and get it."

Corina's Decision

Corina was sitting in the MassageMe offices, pondering what to do with her list. She had a TV on the wall that was broadcasting the news and she was watching a story on the breakout of the H1N1 virus and a murder. She thought, we need to take extra precautions to keep our staff and clients healthy.

Corina decided what to do as the thoughts of influenza and murder sifted through her mind. She was going to call the police and see if she could talk to someone. Making that call from the office was probably not the best thing to do. Picking up her belongings, she checked to make sure the phone was in her pocket along with the list. She told the girls at the front desk that she would return after making a bank deposit. Corina headed to the police station, deciding that she needed to talk to a detective in person, lest they think she was a kook. She could give them the list and describe her concerns.

Corina was sitting in the office of a homicide detective. She had told her story at the front desk, and that officer put her back here. Corina was thinking twice about whether this was the best decision she had ever made. A different officer came in and introduced herself as Detective Liam.

"Hi, my name is Gisela Liam. I am a homicide detective. I gather from what the officer at the front desk told me you think there is something going on at your place of employment."

"Ay, dios mio, si I am the manager at MassageMe in the Gables. I got an intuition and looked into the clients that had not come back to our offices."

"How exactly did you get this intuition, and what is it?"

"An intuition is when you think something might happen."

The officer smiled. "Yes, I am perfectly aware of what intuition is. I mean what is your intuition that brought you here to our station?"

"I am very nervous. I was called by two people who said that one of our clients would not be returning because they died. I understand people die, but it is very odd to have so many people not coming back for massages."

"I am not sure what you are telling me. Do you think you have people dying because they are getting massages?"

"Si, well I don't know. Maybe."

The officer went around the desk and sat beside Corina. "Tell me Ms Corina, why do you think this is happening?"

"I don't know. But I have a list of people. We have one massage therapist the people don't like too well because she talks too much with them. They say she is nosy about their money and their family. I move them when they complain. When you look at this list you will see that many of the people who have not returned are her clients. Also, several on the list live in one or two senior communities in our neighborhood. We have arrangements with them to provide a discount to their residents. We have many who take advantage of that. Maybe there is nothing and I have bothered you for no reason. I will go. I am sorry to take your time, detective."

Detective Liam placed a hand on Corina's arm. "You do not have to go. I believe your concern, and I want to investigate this list. May I see it?"

"Yes, here it is. You can see that the therapists Charleen Parker and Harold Pinter have many of the clients who have not returned. Some of the clients were Charleen's and moved to another when they complain."

Detective Liam moved to the desk. "Just a moment. Let me run a couple of these names and see if they are on any of our lists. Please stay where you are."

Corina nodded in understanding and continued to nervously twist the handkerchief in her hands. The detective took a seat and typed in the first name and saw that person was deceased and on a list the coroner was investigating. She continued through the list and saw that many of the people were on the coroner's list being investigated by the DSA for potential arsenic poisoning.

Detective Liam went back and sat beside Corina. "It is good that you brought this list to us. May I make a copy?"

"You can keep it. I can get another if I need it. I prefer not to have it in my office because if there is something going on, I do not want the therapists to know that I suspect anything. What should I do, detective?"

"Corina, I know this will not be easy, but you will have to act as if you don't know this information. You will need to keep things running at the office the same as they have been. I will be back in touch with you if I need more information."

Corina got up to leave, thanking the officer. She decided not to go back to the office. She was not sure she could pretend that she did not know anything.

Oh, No!

Charleen arrived at the MassageMe early, hoping to get Harold to the storeroom again for a quickie before they had to start their evening. She couldn't express her feelings for him in terms of love; it was more lust, she believed. She was waffling between wanting to run away with him and wanting him to disappear because it was getting complicated. She expected the relationship to go wrong, because they always did. Her girlfriends all told her stories about what happened to women who fooled around with married men. None of the stories ended well for the women.

Charleen shifted thoughts from Harold to her Aunt Betty since the memory of the letter arriving from the attorney had popped into her head.

How could Betty think it was okay to leave all that money to the Foundation for the Blind when she died? Effectively she had cut Charleen out of her will. What had Aunt Betty said during their conversation? "You can take care of yourself. There are many people in this world who can't. I want to leave all my money to them." She had been getting that money moved into her account, but that stupid robot was too hard to manage. It was too bad that Aunt Betty had to die.

Harold interrupted Charleen's thoughts as he walked into the room. He looked ill. There was another therapist in the room, so Charleen was obliged to put on her best professional face.

"Hi, Harold. It's good to see you."

Harold looked at her sadly. "Hello, Charleen. It is good to see you. My wife Mary will be quickly visiting later to have dinner with me here in the lunchroom. She wanted to meet my colleagues that I stayed with last night after the bar."

Charleen paled. "Oh, are they working tonight? I didn't know you had gone out with them last night."

"I tried to tell her that they weren't working, but she said she was coming to bring me dinner anyway. I'll try to make it brief."

The other therapist prepared to leave the room to get to his client. He looked at Harold and Charleen and nodded as he left.

Charleen looked into Harold's eyes. "My next client doesn't get here for another half hour. I came in early. I was certain you would be here. I want to talk about last night. Let's go to the back room."

"I can't. My next client will be here in ten minutes. I need to prepare the room. I am glad I got to warn you about Mary. She asked me if I am having an affair. I think you should stay in your room and stay out of here when she arrives. I'll text you when she is gone. She is coming around six."

Stomping away, Charleen went to her assigned room for the evening to prepare. She was seething. "I knew this would happen. It never works out. What am I going to do? That wife needs to go."

Mary arrived at the MassageMe offices. Harold greeted her and walked her back to the staff offices. He took her the long way, so he didn't have to pass Charleen's room.

Mary looked around and asked, "Are you going to give me a tour of your work?"

"There really isn't much to see. All the rooms are in use, so this is pretty much it."

Mary sat at the table and started to take Chinese food boxes out of a bag.

"Harold, sit down and let's eat. I hope I'll be able to meet your colleagues and thank them for putting you up last night when you were too drunk to drive home."

Harold responded, indicating he was a little more than irritated, "I told you this morning, when you asked, that they both had today off. Thus, the reason they were able to go out drinking last night. I don't usually eat with anyone. I do not know that there will be anyone in the office for you to meet. You met Tracy up front. That's probably all for today."

Just then Charleen walked in. The green returned to Harold's face.

"Hello, I'm Charleen. Harold said you were coming in today. It's a pleasure to meet you. Harold speaks of you all the time. Harold, here is your water bottle. You left it in the room. I knew you were eating with your lovely wife and thought you might want it to share with her."

Harold threw up a little in his mouth; he swallowed. "Thank you Charleen. This is my wife, Mary."

"Mary, it's a pleasure to meet you. Please excuse me; I need to get back to my client."

Charleen started to leave the room.

"It is a pleasure to meet you. Do you also go drinking with Harold?" Mary asked.

Charleen stopped in her tracks and turned back to Mary. "I have been known to go out with the rest of the therapists a time or two. So, I guess the answer is yes, I also go drinking with Harold."

Mary stood up, facing Charleen directly. "Did you go last night?"

Charleen looked at Harold and then to Mary. "No, I did not. I went home to my condo after I left the office. It was a long day, and I just wanted to be at home. I understand the boys tied one on, so to speak. Excuse me, I need to get my next client. Enjoy your dinner; it was lovely to meet you." Charleen turned and left.

Mary looked at Harold. "That's who you are having the affair with, isn't it?"

"Mary, please sit down. I am not having an affair with anyone. How long have we been married?"

"That is the point, Harold; we have been married a long time and I know you very well. It's over, the little affair you are having with her. I am your wife. You need to stop the affair and remember the things I know."

Mary turned to go. Harold watched her walk out the door. This was not the time or the place to go after her. He was also not sure that he wanted to. He couldn't help it; he was hard and wanted to take Charleen and release all his tension into her. He wanted to plead with Charleen for a quickie in the back room now, but he knew she was with a client. He sat back down to eat the dinner that Mary brought. He might as well not let it go to waste and maybe if he concentrated on something else, this boner would go away. He finished his meal. He finished the tea that he put into his water bottle earlier. He filled the container with water and got ready for the next client. The rest of the evening passed quietly.

Charleen handed Harold a note saying that she hoped he would join her at her place after work. Harold tucked it in his pocket as he prepared to finish his last client. His hopes were raised as he thought about the way he would pleasure himself and Charleen in a little over an hour. Harold cleaned up his space at the end of the shift and looked around the office for Charleen. She was already gone. He went to his car and turned it in the direction of Charleen's condo.

When he arrived, Charleen was waiting for him. She was in a gown similar to the see-through gown he imagined her in, that afternoon she came to him in his fantasy. He reached for her and pulled her to him. He was hard and waiting for release. Charleen quieted him and placed her mouth around him. She licked and sucked and he felt the release coming. He pulled her to him and kissed her passionately, slipping his tongue between her teeth, and tasting the sweet flavor of her lips. Then he felt a pain in his leg and his head, and tried to move but he could not. Charleen was gone. It was dark and he did not recognize her condo. For the second time that day, he felt like he was going to throw up, right before he lost consciousness.

Odorless, Colorless and Tasteless

Kathy was sitting at her desk in the DSA offices. She had just gotten the report on the champagne that was left in front of Sarah's house. The technician said, "There is a boatload of thallium in that bottle," when Kathy stopped by the desk that morning to see if anything had been found. Kathy had told the technicians to look for thallium because Sarah had hypothesized thallium as a potential that few people would think about.

Kathy also received a call from a Miami-Dade homicide detective explaining that she had gotten a list of people from the manager at a MassageMe. The interesting thing about the list was that there were people on it who matched the potential arsenic victims. The detective faxed the list to Kathy and that was lying on her desk. The phone rang and for a change Kathy answered.

"Good morning. This is Detective Doe; who am I speaking to?"

"Detective Doe, this is Joanna, the hospital administrator at Mercy. I want to inform you that we have two individuals who are in the intensive care unit that may have been poisoned. They don't match the profile of any of the others though. They are young. One is a man and one is a woman. They were brought in two nights ago."

"When it rains it pours. Joanna, what kind of testing has been done on them?"

Joanna responded, "I don't know but I will check."

"Do that, but I doubt that they were tested for thallium. I have reason to believe it is not arsenic but thallium that is the poison. It's a hunch. I will be there shortly. Where will you be?"

"Come to the hospital administration offices and ask for me. I will tell my assistant to bring you to my office as soon as you arrive."

"Thank you, Joanna. I will see you shortly." Kathy put the phone down. Wow, there was a lot going on in this case. It was not a cut and dry murder.

Kathy: Where are you? Can you meet me at the office?

Sarah's phone buzzed and she recognized Kathy's ringtone.

Sarah called. "Did the results come back on the champagne? What about the dog food? I guess it would be too soon for the dog food. I can come to the office but let me take Chloe out. I was hoping you were Dirk when the text came through."

"Hold on, Sarah, and slow down. I think you should come here, and I will fill you in on everything that I know. How long will it take you to get here?"

"Depends on how long it takes Chloe to pee. I am not letting her in the backyard. The food thing is scary."

"You should keep her out of the backyard. I agree. Just get here when you can. I'll buzz you in when you get here."

Sarah took Chloe for a walk on their usual route. She was about half a mile down the road when she ran into a person in a hoodie. Chloe started barking and lunging at the individual. Sarah could barely hold on to her. The person looked at Sarah and turned and went in the other direction. Chloe calmed down when the person was out of sight. Sarah turned around and went back to the house as she was a bit shaken by the experience. Chloe had never behaved like that when another person had gotten close. She took the leash off Chloe and filled her water dish, then headed out the door. "Guard the house, girl; I'll be back in time for dinner."

Sarah arrived at the DSA offices in record time. Kathy buzzed her into the building. Sarah got off the elevator asking questions before Kathy could even say hello.

"Come to my office first. We'll cover a few things and then we need to go to Mercy Hospital. Apparently, there are two people who may have been poisoned. Joanna the administrator called because based on their admission to the emergency department, the physicians could not rule out food poisoning or some other kind of poison."

Sarah looked at Kathy seriously. "Oh, that is awful. Are they the same profile as the others?"

"No, they are young. I told the administrator to have the physician look for thallium."

Sarah looked questioningly at Kathy because despite thinking that thallium might be the poison, she didn't want to send a physician on a wild goose chase.

"Why did you tell her that? It is just a theory I have. We don't have any evidence."

"Actually, we do. That bottle of champagne had thallium in it. The tech used the word boatload, but I don't think that's an actual technical term."

"I'd laugh if it weren't so serious. What if I liked champagne and we had opened that bottle? I might be the one in the hospital."

"You aren't going to like this either. The dog food has thallium in it. You will need to watch Chloe and maybe take her to the vet."

"I don't think she actually ate any of the food. She barked at it when we went in the yard. Thallium doesn't have an odor to people, but maybe somehow it smelled bad to her. On our walk today, she lunged at someone who was coming toward us in a hoodie. I could not see the person's face. They went the other way when Chloe lunged. I wonder if that is the person that put the food in the backyard or maybe has been around the house?

This is getting very creepy. How do you do your job and not be scared?"

"Well, most of the time, they aren't trying to poison me or my dog, that's how. Let's head to the hospital."

The Accident

The ambulance arrived at the scene of the accident. It appeared that the driver had gone off the road and hit the traffic light post. The Miami-Dade County sheriff had covered the car so that the body was not visible to those passing by. Another sheriff was directing traffic around the accident. The first officer on the scene took the paramedics to the car. The driver door was wrapped around the pole. It took the firemen time to get the car moved before the paramedics could get to the driver. The officer said he didn't know how anyone could be alive, but he was hopeful. He told the paramedics that he had not gotten a response when he banged on the front window or the passenger side of the car. The officer ran the tags on the car and identified the driver. The car belonged to a Harold Pinter of Miami.

This Can't Be Happening

Charleen was calling the law offices of Baronsky and Hart to follow up on the letter she received. She was placed on hold and told that Matt Kline would take her call. When Matt got on the phone he said, "Hello Ms Parker. What can I do for you today?" That question was almost enough to send Charleen over the edge. She was in a bad mood because Harold had not shown up last night and he had not answered her calls.

"I'll tell you why I am calling. I got a certified letter that said that there will be no settlement. It is my understanding from my conversations with Mr Baronsky that he guarantees a settlement. That is why the fee is so high. Why can't I get a settlement from the BOT company for my aunt's death that they caused?"

"Well, Ms Parker, there is no evidence that the BOT company is responsible. They came to meet with us. Mr Baronsky worked them over, but they were not willing to make a settlement payment without evidence. In fact, we have not had a chance to notify you, but there is a counter lawsuit. They are suing the estate for a half a million dollars for the robot."

Charleen turned red, her breathing became shallow, and she sat down before she continued. "This can't be happening; everything is going wrong, so wrong." She just wanted what was due to her, and for all the other jilted family members out there in the world.

Matt Kline was on the other end of the phone saying, "Ms Parker, are you there? Ms Parker. We need to talk about this, I don't believe you will be held responsible since none of the estate went to you. Ms Parker, are you there?"

Charleen was not listening. She dropped the phone. She saw the news media reporting on an accident at the corner of her street. She was sure she recognized the car. How could things get any worse? Charleen ran out of the door of her condo and headed toward the corner. She was stopped by the police officers and forced to stand behind a line of caution tape. It seemed that the men were just getting the driver out of the car. Charleen watched and thought, he is the love of my life. We are supposed to spend the rest of our lives together.

Charleen broke down in tears when they pulled the man from the car. She recognized him and realized that they would not be fulfilling any of the dreams they had together. She backed from the area and ran to her condo. She threw anything and everything that wasn't too heavy or bolted down. She screamed. Nothing was helping her feel better. The weight of the last two years, and the actions she had taken, were too much for her. She wondered how to end her misery. Charleen took deep breaths to calm herself and to think. There was a lot to resolve. Now, she didn't care. She did not even care if everyone found out what she had done. She was grief-stricken. She was so mad at Harold for letting his wife go to the office. She realized through her grief, that in all her life, Harold was the only person who ever cared for her, about her, or who ever really loved her. Her chance at any happiness just died at the corner of Salzedo Street in Coral Gables, Florida. Charleen looked in the mirror. She didn't like the person looking back. She peered at her reflection and sneered, "When did I turn into you?"

I Will Find Who Did This!

Dave, Greta, Pat and China were sitting in the family waiting room close to the ICU. They had taken turns going home and taking showers and then returning. It had been an exceptionally long couple of days. There was no good news. Neither Dirk nor Gina was awake, and the physicians did not provide any glimmer of hope; they just said, "Only time will tell."

"Dave, did you get a hold of Dirk's parents?" Greta asked.

"Yes, I did. It is not easy to tell a mom that her son is in the ICU. They are both well, but traveling is rough for them with his father's Parkinson's disease. His mom said she is going to try and figure out how to get here."

China looked up from her phone. "Did anyone call Gina's mom? I can call her if you want."

Pat shook her head. "I tried to call her, but I haven't been able to get a response. It may be because she doesn't recognize my number. I haven't wanted to leave a message."

China got up. "I'll go make a call to her now. She will answer my number. I'll be back in a few moments. Does anyone want anything from the cafeteria? I am hungry too."

Everyone gave China a thank you but no shake; she headed out to call Gina's mom.

Sarah and Kathy arrived at the hospital and headed toward the administration offices. They were met by the assistant and taken directly to meet with Joanna Smart, the hospital director. Joanna looked up from her desk and motioned for them to take a seat while she finished an email. Sarah and Kathy took a seat. Joanna looked up from her desk and pled with the women, "Please make it stop!"

Kathy and Sarah asked at the same time, "Stop what exactly?"

Joanna sighed. "People dying in my hospital from poison."

"We are doing our best," Kathy replied.

Sarah took her cue from Kathy that she needed to provide some information. "Joanna, it seems that it is not all premeditated poisoning. We discovered that the staff from a food pantry in the area were distributing grape and apple juice that had high concentrations of arsenic."

Joanna sat aghast and could not even find the words to respond to Sarah.

Sarah continued, "I know that is hard to believe. It's not immediately dangerous to adults unless you drink a large quantity. It can be more dangerous to children. We are working with the food pantry director to manage the issue. I have been investigating what other kinds of poisons might be used, as all the cases on our list do not involve arsenic. I considered thallium and brought the idea to Detective Doe. It seems that we now have concrete evidence to support thallium as a likely poison for about half of the individuals that have died." Sarah looked back at Kathy.

Kathy picked up the conversation. "That is why I told you to have the physicians check your two individuals in the ICU. Do you know if they have that in progress?"

"I spoke with them and they sent samples to be tested specifically for thallium. They indicated that a heavy metal tox screen is also in progress or is complete."

"Good. There is a cure for thallium poisoning. It might be prudent to have the physicians start it now, if possible, even before the results come back. They may also need to do hemodialysis, which is a process to clean the blood," explained Sarah.

"We are going to want to talk to the physicians and any family members of the victims," Kathy specified.

"Of course. I can take you to the ICU to speak to the physician. I believe that there are family members or friends of both victims who have been in the family waiting room. I only know they are here because we have had to keep the news media from bothering them. I suppose you saw the trucks outside when you came in," Joanna said. "Why are they here? Is it the H1N1 outbreak?" Kathy said as she looked out the window to where Joanna pointed.

"No, apparently one of the victims owns a company and it was leaked to the press. I suppose it is about stock prices, but I wish they would just go home. We try to keep them in a certain area, but they keep making their way to the floor trying to find someone to talk to." Joanna stood up, moving toward the door and indicated that Sarah and Kathy should follow. They arrived in the ICU and introductions were made. Kathy asked the physicians a few questions about the admission. She then turned it over to Sarah. "This is Doctor Sandling. She is working on this case with me. She is a pharmacist. I believe she has identified with a high probability the kind of poison that is being used. We have not figured out how everything ties together but we are getting close. Sarah, go ahead and discuss what you mentioned earlier."

"Hi, I'm Sarah. It's good to meet you. I think we are dealing with thallium."

The ICU physician asked, "Why do you think that? It isn't even in the heavy metal toxicology screens."

Sarah paused patiently before speaking. "We have been working on this case for several weeks. We have been through a list of heavy metal and plant possibilities. Based on the symptoms of the other people who were admitted with flu-like symptoms, high potassium, leg pain and nail bed changes, I narrowed it down to a couple of substances. Thallium is one. It is available here in South Florida because of the use in semi-conductor manufacturing and the OptyX company also uses it in the production of glasses. It is colorless, odorless, tasteless and can be absorbed through the skin. I am not sure yet why I think that last part about the skin is important, but I am sure it is."

"Do you have a recommendation for treating them, since you are sure it is thallium?"

"Actually, I do. The treatment is not harmful if it isn't thallium and so nothing is lost. But if it is thallium, then you have gained time and potentially a quicker time to recovery. If the lab comes back that it is not thallium, then you can stop the Prussian blue that I recommend. Is it possible to give the patients anything by mouth?"

The nurse spoke up. "We can't give them anything by mouth now. They are intubated."

Sarah considered. "If it is thallium, they will need Prussian blue for a couple months. The capsules can be opened but that will not help while they have a tube down their throat that goes to their lungs. I expected that I might be asked to speak to you, and so I looked to see what other treatment options are available. It seems that you can do charcoal hemoperfusion or hemodialysis to clean the blood. Hopefully, that will help enough that they will wake up or at least not need to be on a respirator. It seems those are the best options for treatment. In the meantime, it might be helpful to speak to the pharmacist for the ICU and get them to order Prussian blue so that when the individuals are awake, they can be started on it immediately."

The physician shook hands with Kathy and Sarah and thanked them. He spoke to the nurse and put in an order for hemodialysis for both patients. Kathy looked at Sarah and mouthed, "Thank you."

"Thank you for what? It's what I am trained to do."

"Yes, but not like this. It has been quite an adventure. I am glad we are on it together."

"Well, it isn't over until the fat lady sings and we need to find the fat lady."

Kathy just laughed. "Joanna went to take care of something else. She told me that we will find the friends and family of the two patients in the waiting room. She said it is quiet and we can speak in there."

The women headed to the family room. Upon entering, Sarah and Kathy looked around and there was only one older woman waiting. Kathy introduced herself to the woman. It was apparent the woman had been crying. She looked at Kathy. "I have already spoken to the police. I don't know what more I can tell you. I should have just thrown that basket away."

Sarah sat down next to the woman. "I am sorry. It must be very hard. Is it your family members that may have been poisoned? I am Sarah; I'm a pharmacist. We are with a special part of the police that investigates crimes that deal with drugs, or chemicals."

Through tears, the woman said, "Hi, I am Greta; I am the assistant for the CEO of the BOT company."

Sarah gasped. "Is it Dirk that has been poisoned?"

Greta looked at Sarah skeptically. "Yes, but who are you?"

"I am the girl with the dog Chloe. We were supposed to go on a date last night, but he didn't text me back. I thought he stood me up, but I did make allowances for missing the date if he was lying in a hospital bed. I just didn't know it was the truth when I said it."

Greta began sobbing and leaned over on Sarah's shoulder. Sarah put her arm around Greta's shoulders. "Please can you just tell us what happened?"

China came in the door, talking to Dave. She stopped in her tracks and stared at the women. She gained her composure. "How did you know to come here?"

Sarah and Kathy looked at China and nothing came together at all about this story.

"China, we are investigating a poisoning. I think we just found out that it is Dirk that is here and has been poisoned," Sarah said.

China sighed. "Yes, Sarah, and Gina too."

The women could not hide their shock.

Dave, Greta, and China all provided different parts of the story as Kathy and Sarah listened. Neither Kathy nor Sarah had anything to say throughout the story; they were left speechless.

Kathy finally asked the obvious question. "Do you have any idea who or why?"

Dave took the lead on this question. "We have been wracking our brains. We have no idea. We circled around to considering the person who instigated the lawsuit, but we don't even know who that person is."

Sarah looked to Dave as she stood up. "Can I see Dirk?"

"I don't see why not. Maybe if he hears your voice it will trigger recovery. He says he is going to marry you."

Now it was Sarah who stopped in her tracks. She merely smiled at Dave and headed back to the ICU and was directed to the room where Dirk was lying. She looked around at all the monitors and checked his blood pressure and heart rate. She saw that his heart rhythm was normal. Those are all good signs, she thought. She took his hand in hers. She squeezed his hand. "So, I was a little upset that you stood me up last night. I told Kathy you better have a good excuse. This is an exceptionally good excuse. I promise you can make it up to me. I'll be back to see you every day. I am going to help Kathy find the person that did this to you."

Sarah put the bed rail down so she could reach Dirk's face. She laid her hand on his forehead and ran her fingers through his hair. She gave him a little kiss on the cheek. She put the bedrail back in position and left the room, determined to find the person that did this.

Discovery

Tim kept the BOT offices open with the assistance of Jessie Smith. Most of the staff were coming to the office every day, but some continued to work from home. They expressed fear over being in the office. Tim was checking in with Dave several times a day. Dave reported this morning that both Dirk and Gina were breathing on their own and were being given an antidote for the poison. They would be moved to regular rooms sometime during the day.

Tim told Dave that he called the Foundation for the Blind in Dallas to see if he could advance his knowledge about the niece of Betty Carmichael. Tim related this story to Dave. "The woman at the Foundation said that Betty Carmichael contacted her about a year before she died. Betty wanted to arrange to leave all her estate, including proceeds from her house, to the Foundation. Betty started to make regular payments to the Foundation after that discussion to support their operating costs. The support was being issued from the EYE BOT each month as a direct deposit. Betty spoke highly of the EYE BOT program and said she didn't know how she managed without it in all the years before. She emphasized that she wanted some proceeds to be used to provide EYE BOTS to others with vision impairment if they could not afford one. Then about six months before Betty died, the direct deposits stopped. The staff from the Foundation attempted to contact Betty, but the niece Caly Parker intervened. Caly told the staff that there would be no more support for the Foundation and that they should not count on receiving money from the estate. Caly indicated that her aunt had changed her mind. The woman from the Foundation went on to say that Betty must have discovered that her niece was interfering and had stopped the payments because Betty called about three months before she died and gave specific instructions for a Foundation staff member to pick up a notarized signed copy of her last will and testament, that could not be contested, that same day. The fire at the house was a shock to all at the Foundation, but the bigger shock was the death of Betty." Tim asked, "Are you still there, Dave?"

Dave responded, "Yes, still here, but that is quite the story."

"Right? That's what I was thinking when the woman was telling me."

"I am not sure I should ask if there is more."

"There is. There is speculation around the Foundation office that Caly poisoned her aunt. No one could get anyone to investigate it though. Apparently, the word from the neighbor is that Betty came down with symptoms of the flu, and she was saying that she had pain in her legs. That went on for about a month, and Betty didn't get better, only worse. The neighbor tried to get her to the hospital when she first started having symptoms, but Betty kept saying it was a cold and would go away. When Betty finally went and was admitted to the hospital, she died a couple of days later. How freaky is that?"

"Pretty freaky, Tim."

"Guess what else?"

"I am afraid to ask."

"I went back over the records. The time that the EYE BOT went offline corresponds with the timeline the woman at the Foundation gave me. That means the niece must know where the BOT is."

Dave was rubbing his forehead, trying to keep a headache at bay. He said to Tim, "That is a lot of information to process. Did you talk to the neighbor?"

"No, that is all information from the woman at the Foundation. Betty had the neighbor's help for many things. So, the neighbor is the one that took her to the hospital and informed them at the Foundation when Betty died."

"Excellent work. Now we need to find this Caly Parker."

"Well, I have a lead on that too. She is in South Florida. I am just not sure where, yet."

Dave coughed. "Excuse me? What did you say?"

"She is here in South Florida. Do you think she is the one behind the lawsuit? Maybe she is, and when she found out we countersued she tried to poison Dirk."

Dave sat back in his chair. He didn't quite know what to do with all the information he had just gotten from Tim.

"Doctor Johnson, what do you want me to do next?"

"Nothing. Thank you, Tim. I do not want you to get any closer than you already are. There is a lot going on here. I don't want anyone else in the company to be in danger. I am going to give the information you have shared with me just now to the police. They may be in contact with you. Provide them with anything they need. Thank you, Tim, excellent work. You make a great detective."

Dave pulled out the card that Kathy had given him before she left the hospital. He sent a text.

Dave: Detective, this is Dave Johnson. I have some interesting news. Please call.

I Know Who it Is!

Kathy and Sarah were sitting in the DSA office. Chloe was at their feet gnawing on a fake bone. They were reviewing all the information that they had collected. Kathy remembered the list that came from the manager at MassageMe. She pulled it out and handed it to Sarah. She reviewed the list and compared it with their list of deceased individuals.

"Eleven of the people on the list from the MassageMe had one therapist named Parker. There are eight people of the eleven that live in the same community as Ruth Morgan. There is one that lives there that had the therapist named Pinter."

Kathy paused her search, looking up at Sarah. "This could be the common thread. I think I should find out if all these people had large estates. We already know that Ruth Morgan did. Maybe there is a relationship between someone from the assisted living community staff and the hospital. That could make your earlier thoughts valid."

Sarah thought for a moment before responding. "Do you know why the manager brought the list to the police? Does she think that a massage therapist is killing people?"

Kathy replied, "That is what the officer that contacted me implied. How can that happen?"

"With a poison that can be absorbed through the skin and builds up over time. A person would not die immediately after a massage and it might take several massages depending on how the therapist puts it on the individual. The therapist might think there is little chance of being caught. The therapist would have to be careful to not absorb the poison on their own skin. Theoretically it could happen like that. The question I have is why is a massage therapist killing little old ladies who have money? That is the key, isn't it? The money. People kill for revenge, money or love; isn't that what you told me?"

Kathy nodded her head yes as she looked at a text that she just received. She read it and showed it to Sarah.

Sarah gasped. "What are you waiting for?"

Kathy called Dave and she and Sarah listened to the story that he unfolded. Dave told them about the Betty Carmichael missing EYE BOT, her death, and the lawsuit. He told them about Caly Parker. Kathy asked him a couple more questions about what happened at the office and the basket that he had mentioned previously.

Dave remembered the note. "There was the strangest note with the basket. It was written in Latin and basically said carpe diem and whatever else means for tomorrow is uncertain. Right now, my brain won't remember the words."

Kathy and Sarah looked at each other for a moment. Sarah took a deep breath. "Dave, this is Sarah. Are you sure that is what the note said?"

Dave responded, "Absolutely, it was kind of ominous."

Sarah pulled her hair back nervously into a ponytail. "Dave, the same person tried to poison me and Chloe."

Now it was Dave's turn to be stunned into silence.

Kathy looked at Sarah, and she said to Dave, "Do you know where this Caly Parker lives?"

Dave replied, "Tim found that she moved here to South Florida, but he hasn't been able to locate her yet."

"Tell him to back down. I don't want him to be in danger."

"Already done. Are you two coming to the hospital later? Well actually, Sarah are you coming because Dirk is asking for you."

Sarah blushed. "Tell him I'll be there later."

Kathy hung up the phone.

Sarah asked, "Now what?"

"We need to go back through the evidence." She recounted the facts and theories. "We have several victims of supposed poisoning. Some of them are not victims of murder but have inadvertently been poisoned by drinking too much grape and apple juice. We have taken care of that problem at the local level but have more to do. Some of the people who died were infected with influenza or the H1N1 virus and the right testing was not done at the right time to determine which one. That leaves us with about a dozen, mostly seventyish year-old women who were potentially killed by a massage therapist for a reason we don't know; or they were killed by someone at their assisted living community, or Mercy Hospital staff, for their money. Next, we know for certain that someone tried to kill you and Chloe with thallium. No one knows that you are working on this case unless it is someone inside the DSA. You didn't tell your mother, right?"

Sarah laughed. "Are you kidding? She would faint dead away."

"Just checking to make sure that no one outside of the DSA but us, and the people we are talking to know of your involvement. What about your class?"

"I don't think they believed me when I said I am writing a crime novel. But I did not share that I am working with you."

Kathy continued. "We know for certain that someone tried to kill the CEO of BOT Corp and that Gina was a side casualty. We know that the same method was used, a gift of drink and food, to try and poison you, Chloe and Dirk."

"It can't be a jealous girlfriend. We only went out once. Wait, what did Dave say the name of that niece is?"

"Caly Parker."

Sarah, stunned, stood up. "Oh my gosh. It's Charleen. No, I must have it all wrong; that's impossible."

"What are you talking about?"

Sarah began to ramble through her thoughts. "Do you remember the other day when I said that Charleen asked me about Chloe? I never told the class that I had a dog. I thought it was odd, but decided well, maybe I did tell them. But I am sure I did not. I got a little suspicious that she was being too nice. I played along, but here is the part that just gave me chills. When she left the classroom, I heard someone ask, Caly, are you coming? I didn't know who they were talking to at the time. It had to be Charleen. That must be a nickname. Oh, this is so not good. Charleen is a massage therapist. That is how it all ties together. But why would she want to kill a bunch of sweet little old ladies who are leaving their money to charity? How would she know? This is crazy."

"Sarah, Sarah, breathe. You are not breathing. You are just talking. What are you talking about?"

Sarah looked at Kathy. She took a deep breath, and then she took another. "Charleen Parker, the massage therapist in my class, is the killer and the man Pinter is the husband from the couple we met that one day at the Iguana that Chloe growled at."

"Why don't you take Chloe out? She looks like she needs a break. I am going to make a phone call."

"Something you don't want me to hear?"

"No, look at Chloe; she needs to go out. I don't want to waste time. I am going to see if I can get the manager at the MassageMe. I am going to find out if it is indeed a Charleen Parker on that list of therapists. Then I am going to call the prosecutor's office and get a warrant for her arrest."

Sarah and Chloe headed back in after their break. Kathy was still on the phone. They sat down and waited to see what was happening. Kathy got off the phone. "The manager is not comfortable speaking on the phone from that office. She is going to meet us here in about an hour."

Sarah looked uneasy. "Charleen may have a hot temper but I really am having trouble believing this. Do you mind if I take Chloe and go see Dirk? She is trained as a therapy dog so I can call the volunteer coordinator at the hospital and see if we can go together. I'll visit Dirk and Gina and then I'll be back here by the time the manager gets here."

"I think that is an excellent idea."

How Romantic of You

Sarah and Chloe stopped to see the volunteer coordinator at the hospital and say hello. They got permission for Chloe to visit Dirk. They headed to the general medicine floor where both Dirk and Gina were still being treated. Sarah and Chloe arrived at Dirk's room. She peeked in to make sure it was okay for her to enter. Dirk waved her in. Sarah was immediately taken in by his smile. It was what captured her attention on the street, and it was what drew her into his world when she looked at him now. "Sarah, I am so sorry I missed our date," he said.

Sarah laughed. "Really, that is what you are worried about? Someone just tried to kill you and Gina, and you want to apologize?"

"I understand that we have you to thank for saving our skin. Thank you."

"I would do the same for anyone, but I am glad I could save your skin, as you say."

"Did you come talk to me when I was in the ICU? I thought I heard you, but I was somewhere else."

"I did come in and see you and told you I was going to catch whoever did this to you."

Dirk chuckled. "How romantic of you. Don't you think you should let the police do that? By the way, how did you know what we were poisoned with so you could suggest a treatment?"

Sarah giggled quietly. "I will fill you in on the answer to both questions, but today is not that day. I am only glad that you are recovering, and so is Chloe." Chloe walked over and licked Dirk's hand that he put out for her. Dirk patted her head and then suppressed his smile and got serious.

"Dave told me that you and Chloe were also poisoned."

"We weren't poisoned. There was an attempt. We are fine. Can I get you anything?"

Dirk got a playful look on his face and said, "I know I don't know you very well, but there is something you can give me. You can give me another one of those kisses like the other day in the ICU only you missed my lips."

Sarah blushed. "I thought you were out of it."

"I was but like I said, I heard you like you were coming through a fog. I didn't know what you were saying, but I felt your touch; I knew it was you. I knew I had to come back to the world to see you."

She put down the bed rail. She leaned over and brushed her fingers through his hair, and this time she did not miss his lips. Chloe barked, 'woof'.

"I'll be out of here tomorrow. I'll text you," said Dirk.

Sarah blew a kiss as she walked out the door. Sarah and Chloe headed down the hall to check on Gina before they needed to leave. She gave a soft knock on the door and heard Dave say, "Come in."

Gina looked up and smiled. "Hi, Sarah. So, this is the infamous Chloe? I understand I have you to thank for saving Dirk's and my life."

Sarah felt the color rise in her face. "I didn't save your life. The physicians would have figured it out."

"I think you are being way too modest. Thank you too," said Dave.

"I am glad you and Dirk are both recovering. I think we all need a party. But I am betting you won't want wine for a while." Sarah laughed quietly.

Gina laughed, thinking to herself, maybe Sarah and I can be friends. She will be good for Dirk. "Sarah, you are right. I don't think I'll ever have wine and cheese again."

Sarah looked at Gina and could tell she was tired. "We just stopped for a minute. Dirk said you might go home tomorrow. If there is anything you need, well, you have my number." Sarah winked.

Chloe Catches the Killer

Kathy called Sarah as she was leaving the hospital. "Meet me back here at the station. We are going to arrest Charleen Parker. I want Chloe to be with you. If Charleen is the person who dropped that bottle off in front of your house, Chloe will identify her."

"Okay." Sarah pulled out into traffic and headed toward the DSA offices. She was horrified by all that had happened in the last week. She was also a little surprised that she didn't get another text from her mother after she said she would text back but forgot. It'd been busy. She would call her when this was over and tell her she found Dirk. That would make her a happy mom. By the time Sarah had thought through all that had happened, she had arrived back at the DSA. Sarah and Chloe moved over to an official DSA vehicle from her Mustang. Chloe tried to get in the front seat, her usual spot, but Sarah moved her to the back.

Sarah got a 'woof'.

Sarah and Kathy laughed, despite the seriousness of the situation.

"Fill me in. I am sorry I missed the MassageMe manager," said Sarah.

"It's just as well. She was nervous. I thought she might faint from hyperventilation at one point. It is Charleen Parker, the student from your class that is the therapist on the list. Corina is the manager's name. She confirmed your suspicion that Caly is a nickname for Charleen. She started at the MassageMe a little over a year ago. Corina also confirmed that Charleen moved to South Florida from somewhere else about that same time. She told me that women complained about Charleen as a therapist. They said she was nosy and wanted to know about their family and their money and what they were going to do with it. She also told me that Harold Pinter worked there. Corina thinks he was killing people too."

"I knew there was something off that day at the Iguana. Chloe did not like him. How do you know he isn't in on it, or making Charleen do it?"

"Well, if he was, it doesn't matter. Corina said he was killed in an automobile accident within the last week."

Sarah sighed. "This is awful. I wonder what makes people go down this road. I can't imagine taking someone's life. Nothing, not revenge, money or love could make it worth it."

"That's because you have a moral compass. Charleen and many others do not."

The women arrived at the MassageMe. They got out of the car and went in. Sarah took the leash off Chloe. Kathy showed her badge to Tracy at the front desk and said they were looking for Charleen Parker. Tracy pointed to the back. Corina came out of her office and nodded to Kathy and opened the hallway door. Chloe headed down the hall. She stopped at a door and started barking. Kathy knocked on the door. There was no answer. Chloe started jumping up on the door. Kathy didn't get an answer, but it was apparent from Chloe's reaction that someone was in the room. Kathy opened the door. Chloe rushed in first and her bark changed to a growl and she lunged at the individual lying on the table. Sarah quickly grabbed Chloe and leashed her and calmed her down. Kathy went to the table and looked at the woman.

She looked at Sarah. "Is this Charleen Parker?"

Sarah went around the table to look at her face. She put two fingers on the unconscious woman's carotid artery to check for a pulse and said, "Yes, and we need to call 911."

Back at the Café Iguana Meet You

Kathy and Sarah were at the Café Iguana sitting on the patio. Chloe was lying beside the table, watching the crowd walk past. It was a warm, sunny day and the women were relaxed and drinking ice cold beers.

"I can't believe that Charleen tried to kill herself by drinking thallium," said Sarah. "Well, I guess I can. When I was in the hospital room visiting, she told me she looked in the mirror and didn't recognize the monster she had become. She told me that she had an affair with the other therapist on the list, Harold Pinter. She also told me he was killed in an automobile accident and that with him gone she didn't deserve to live. I feel really bad for her."

Kathy looked at Sarah. "You really are too nice. That woman killed at least fifteen people deliberately and slowly in most cases. I don't know how you can feel for her. She could have killed you and Chloe."

Sarah looked sad. "But she didn't. Let's move on to a happier topic. The BOT company is doing great, Dave asked Gina out, and Dirk and I are looking forward to the future. What about you and China?"

Kathy grinned. "I don't know if it will go anywhere. It remains to be seen."

Kathy got a notification and looked at her phone. She looked back at Sarah. "I think this is where we started. It's Doctor Canon."

Epilogue

On a bright sunny day in the spring, Mary buried her husband Harold Pinter's ashes on the outskirts of Euclid, Ohio. For her it was a day of reckoning. Her last words to him had been 'remember what I know'. They should have been 'I love you'. She thought to herself, the best advice she could give her children is to tell them to love each other, their spouses and their children and to share those words freely because you never know when it will be the last time. Mary quit her job the day after the accident. She was moving back to Euclid as soon as the condo in Miami sold. She already had an offer from the first day it went on the market. There was nothing in South Florida for her now that her beloved Harold was gone. She would live with one of their daughters and spend the rest of her life loving her family unconditionally and reminding them of that every day.

Charleen confessed that she used thallium added to lotion to poison the women. She did it because they, like her Aunt Betty, said they were leaving all their money to charity rather than to family. She was arrested and would face trial for the first-degree murder of fifteen individuals, including Betty Carmichael. Other charges filed included the attempted murder of Dexter Irwin

Keene, Gina Portense, Sarah Sandling and her dog Chloe. She was being held in a Miami-Dade County jail awaiting trial. Detective Kathy Doe provided enough evidence to the prosecutor that Charleen would likely never see freedom again.

Sarah was promoted to full professor at the University of Miami in recognition of her work at the university, in the community, and her published manuscripts including the most recent on 'The Roles of Pharmacists in the New Health Care Era' published in the New England Journal of Medicine. Sarah was recognized by the DSA for service to the organization. She was offered a part-time position with the department. The expectations made were that she would serve alongside Detective Doe in solving crimes related to chemicals, medications, plants, and health. It came with a badge. The badge made Sarah happy. She asked if Chloe could have one too. It was Chloe who identified Charleen Parker as the murderer. Sarah self-proclaimed the name of her first case of murder — 'Chloe's Catch'.

Kathy Doe was at the gym one morning without Sarah. She had called China the day before and said she would meet her there. The women met and headed to the workout space. Each considered it the first step toward friendship and exploring the world with each other in it and to see where that adventure might lead.

Dirk called Sarah to thank her for saving his life and Gina's for what Sarah thought must be the hundredth time. She continued to tell him she would have done the same for anyone. Every day for a week he sent a dozen red roses to her house with a card signed, 'Thank you, and I look forward to our future. Will you marry me? Dirk'. Each day, Sarah laughed and sent him a text:

Thank you. Not today, but maybe tomorrow. Love Sarah and Chloe.

Dave had pined for Gina for years. He had kept his distance because he thought Gina always had a thing for Dirk, and he didn't think she knew he existed. During her hospital stay, he was by her bedside almost 24/7 until she regained consciousness and after. During that time, he realized that life is short, and he needed to take a step forward in life and the only person he wanted to do that with was Gina. When she was released from the hospital, he asked her out, and her response was a resounding, "Finally!"

The BOT Corporation received a one-million-dollar investment check from the Foundation for the Blind in honor of their work to advance the independence of persons with vision impairment.

Dr Canon finished with the autopsy he had been working on for the last week. He sat back and reflected on the value of Detective Doe and Dr Sandling to the last investigation. He thought, maybe he could do this for a few more years with those two working with him.

He wrote the autopsy report on the man lying on the table. He sent a text to Detective Doe.

Dr Canon: I need your help. Will you and Dr Sandling be here after lunch? We have a new case.

CPSIA information can be obtained
at www.ICGtesting.com
Printed in the USA
BVHW030351060222
627511BV00008B/5

9 781800 162952